Mary Ashton Rice Livermore

Pen Pictures, or, Sketches From Domestic Life

Mary Ashton Rice Livermore

Pen Pictures, or, Sketches From Domestic Life

ISBN/EAN: 9783337010416

Printed in Europe, USA, Canada, Australia, Japan

Cover: Foto ©Andreas Hilbeck / pixelio.de

More available books at **www.hansebooks.com**

PEN PICTURES:

OR,

SKETCHES FROM DOMESTIC LIFE.

BY

MRS. M. A. LIVERMORE,

———————◦———————

CHICAGO:

S. C. GRIGGS & CO., 39 AND 41 LAKE STREET.

1862.

S. & A. EMERSON, Printers,
174 South Clark Street.

CONTENTS.

THE LIFE-LONG SACRIFICE.

The summer sun had just dipped below
the horizon, leaving its track adown the western sky, glorious and golden. The air was
quivering with the thousand songs of birds,
perfume was beginning to exhale from the
now reviving flowers, and from the valleys
and water-courses a cool mist was wreathing
upward, like the very breath of evening. On
the low door-stone of an humble dwelling,
around which clustered a profusion of red
and white rose-trees, while sweet-briar clambered over the door, and morning-glories and
blue-bells curtained the windows, sat two
children — a brother and sister — both bend-
ing over the same crumbled and torn bit of
newspaper, which they were eagerly reading.
The sister, who might have seen fourteen
summers, and who sat with her arm about
her brother's neck — a lad some two or three
years her junior — was, even at that early
and immature age, a noble and queenly crea-

2

ture. Underneath a broad and massive brow, beamed large, dark, fathomless eyes, that would have given beauty to the homeliest face. Her cheek was clear, and almost transparent; her mouth finely cut, and very sweet in its expression; while from her face there beamed an earnest, wishful, appealing look, mingled with a pensiveness that seemed to indicate that she had already tasted of the bitterness of life. The most careless observer would have perceived, immediately, that the young girl was endowed with remarkable talents; while nicer discriminators would have beheld the lofty powers of soul within that were struggling for development, immense mental energies, restless for lack of employment, and a sensitive, highly gifted spirit, destined to accomplish much of good or evil, as circumstances or fate should decree.

The brother was a being very much after the order of his sister; the same regal brow and glorious eyes bespoke their common parentage. There was on his face a less sorrowful and thoughtful look; for a less sensitive organization was his, and, as yet, his inner nature, unlike his sister's, had not commenced a warfare with his outward circumstances. While he thirsted for knowledge, as for water, he also found delight in the sports of his age, and entered with zest into all the pastimes of boyhood.

They were now seated side by side, unconscious of all around them, eagerly devouring the fragmentary knowledge of the torn paper. It was one of a series of "Letters from the South of Europe," on which they had chanced to light; and, as they followed the *voyageur* through desolated Greece, and storied Rome, and the land of Moorish and Christian valor, their hearts glowed within them, and their countenances became radiant with enthusiasm. And yet, every moment or two, a cloud, a puzzled expression, passed over their faces, and the sister sighed and seemed troubled; and, at last, ere the article was completed, as if vexed to the soul, she pushed the paper from her, and burst out, impatiently and petulantly,—

" Oh, dear! it's of no use to read any further, Henry; we can't understand half we are reading. What is the 'Decameron of Boccaccio;' and who, or what, are Dante, and Ariosto, and Tasso, and Petrarch, and Cervantes? It's nothing but vexation!" And she shrugged her shoulders, and pushed

2B

back the paper, as though greatly annoyed.

"Yes," replied the brother, in the same vexed tone, "and just look here, on the other page, Emily. Here is a 'Critical Notice of Jean Paul Richter,' that we had better not undertake to read. Just look at the names lugged into it — Goethe, Schiller, Klopstock, and — and — but I won't try to pronounce them. It is, as you say, only vexation for us to read anything, for we are everlastingly stumbling over something we don't understand!"

"Only yesterday, when I was reading a simple story in that Philadelphia paper you borrowed, I found something in it about the 'poisoned shirt of Nessus,' and the 'wakeful bird of Pallas,' that spoilt the whole for me. I had as lief try to read Greek."

"And I should like to see the book or paper, that is n't brimful of such names as Lear, Macbeth, Falstaff, Hamlet, and so on; they stare you in the face, let you take up what you may. Do you suppose we shall ever find out what they mean, Emily?"

"Oh dear, I don't know," sighed the sister; "sometimes mother can inform us about what we are ignorant;" and, acting on her own suggestion, she pushed open the door

of the humble room within, that served for
both parlor and kitchen, and leaning back
from the door-step, said, "Mother, Henry
and I are reading an old paper that we 've
found; there is something in it about Petrarch and Laura, and Dante and Beatrice,
and Tasso: can you tell us anything about
them?"

Mrs. Holden rose, with sewing in hand,
and came to the door. She was an uncom-
monly intelligent looking woman, with a
broad, clear, high brow, overhanging her
pale face, which, though full of sweetness,
bore the traces of sorrow and suffering. After seeing the mother, one would cease to
wonder at the noble expansion of brow, the
soul-full eyes, and the expression of loveliness, that marked the children in an unusual
and peculiar manner. She bent over her
daughter for an instant, and then replied:

"No, my dear, I can tell you nothing
about them. There was less thought about
education, when I was young, than there is
now; and my parents, like your mother, were
too poor to send me to school a great deal."

"We cannot understand more than half
we read," said Emily, sorrowfully, "just because of our ignorance."

"If your father had lived," said Mrs. Holden, compassionately, "you would have had opportunities for education that are denied you now. He thought a great deal of a good education."

"Ah me!" sighed Emily, in deep despondency, "if we were only rich!"

The mother made no reply, but a deeper shade of sadness mantled her fine features, and she gazed down sorrowfully on her noble children. A tear trickled silently down the cheek of Emily, another and then another followed, and presently she was in an agony of tears. Mrs. Holden stooped down, and drew her tenderly to her bosom, and while she endeavored to soothe her, mingled her tears with her daughter's. Henry also sought to administer consolation, in an awkward way, and struggled manfully to keep back the tears that from sympathy, would fain have deluged his cheek.

Mrs. Holden allowed her daughter to weep unrestrainedly. When she became calm again, and had raised once more her head from her mother's bosom, her eyelids yet wet with tears, the mother endeavored to speak to the sensitive girl words of contentment and hope.

"You must not lay your poverty and ignorance so sorely to heart, Emily," she said, tenderly. "A way may yet be opened, by which your desires for knowledge will be gratified; make the most of what you have, and that will pave the way for more. 'God helps those who help themselves,' you know."

"Yes, mother," said Emily, her eyes shining through her tears, as if a new thought had flashed into her mind; "there is another saying that I often call to mind: 'Get thy spindle and distaff ready, and God will send the flax.' Now I am sure my spindle and distaff *are* ready," she continued, smiling, "and I am only waiting for the flax."

"Here's another, better than either," said Henry, with animation; "it ought to make us, poor things, pluck up courage. I think of it every day, and I always feel better for remembering it. 'Where there's a will, there's a way!' Now, I'm nothing but a poor boy, to be sure, but I've a great desire to be an educated man; and,—you may smile, mother, as much as you please,—educated I will be! I may be twenty, thirty, or forty years old, before I go to college—but go there I will, if not till I'm old as Methusaleh."

"Yes, and you'll not be thirty, nor yet

twenty years old, before you enter college, poor and humble little boy as you now are!" said Emily, with enthusiasm. "I am *sure* God will provide for us. What did Mr. Eaton say, last Sabbath, in his sermon? 'Has God given us the desire for improvement, and will he not place the means in our power?' That sentence fell into my heart like a ray of sunlight into a dark place. I said to myself, 'Be of good cheer; God has certainly given thee the *desire* for improvement, and in his own good time, He will certainly send thee the *means.*' And I am sure He will, mother; just as sure as though I had heard it promised with an audible voice."

Mrs. Holden looked almost sorrowfully on the rapt face of her enthusiastic child, for she could divine no way by which her darling wish was to be gratified; she forbore, however, to crush the hope that for the moment inspired her, and gradually changed the conversation to other subjects.

During the next few days, both Mrs. Holden and Henry observed that Emily was much occupied in her own thoughts, and conversed even less than usual. She seemed occupied in some scheme or plan of her own, and made several visits to the post-office of the little village, a mile distant. No questions were asked, for Emily seemed to desire secrecy, and Mrs. Holden believed she would eventually confide to her her plans and purposes. Nor was she mistaken. As the good lady sat quietly at work, a few days afterwards, Emily darted up the grassy yard, and, breathless with haste and excitement, held before her mother's eyes a letter, bearing her own address, the very first she had ever received.

"What does that mean?" asked Mrs. Holden, calmly.

"Why, it means, mother, that on Monday I am going to take the first step towards educating myself and Henry," replied Emily, with a glowing cheek, and a dilated eye.

"What, my dear?"

"Well, mother, I empowered Anna Stone, who works in a cotton factory, in Massachusetts, you know, to obtain a situation for me, on her return. Here is her letter, informing me that I must be in Lowell next week."

"But what has that to do with the education of Henry and yourself?"

"Much—everything. After I have earned enough to defray the expense, I shall go, for a time, to some good school—then return to the factory and earn more — further than that, the vision doth not now extend. But I shall surely be guided along in the best way. 'God helps those who help themselves,' you told me, the other night. How do you like my plan?"

"I do not like it at all; for its operation will remove from me my only daughter, will deprive Henry of his only sister, and will consign you to long, weary days of drudgery and ceaseless labor. But I will not oppose it, and in efforts at self-improvement, may God bless you!"

"Oh, a thousand thanks, dear mother! ten thousand, thousand thanks!" and Emily threw her arms alternately about her mother and brother.

"And now, I do verily believe that our prospects are beginning to brighten — that this will be an epoch in our history — that you and I, Henry, can begin to free ourselves from our fetters of ignorance;" and with her brilliant eyes, and glowing cheeks, and dilated figure, she seemed another Pythia, speaking the oracle of a god.

Mrs. Holden smiled at her enthusiasm. "Do not be too sanguine, my dear child! An oak is not felled by one blow. A young girl, like you, cannot expect, in many years, to earn sufficient to defray the expenses of your own and your brother's education."

But Emily still seemed inspired with the largest hope, and she replied, in a tone full of confidence, "We'll see, dear mother, we'll see!"

From her very infancy, Emily Holden had been noticed for her uncommon mental precocity. All bore witness to the fact, that she possessed intellectual gifts worthy the highest culture. But the iron hand of poverty pressed hard upon her. Her father, who was a poor man, had died in her infancy, and Mrs. Holden, whose sole dependence was her husband's labor, was left to rear as she could her infant daughter, and a son a few weeks old. Their residence was in a small, poor, out-of-the-way town, in a state at that time more unfriendly than any other of the New England states to the cause of education. After Emily had advanced to the very highest point that the miserable apology for a school supported by the district could carry her, there seemed an end to all further progress. There was no high school in the town, no private school, and the idea of normal schools was then hardly broached. But it was not in the nature of a mind like Emily's to rest satisfied in ignorance. She was constantly in quest of knowledge; and, unfavorable as were her circumstances, not a day passed that she did not add to her slender stock of facts and ideas.

The feverish and inordinate thirst of her spirit for progress being ungratified, she became restless, moody, and discontented. Already life had become a mystery to her; there were times when it was distasteful; her spiritual aspirations were so at variance with her outward circumstances, that she sometimes wondered what there was in life pleasing, and looked wearily forward to the years of the future. The ordinary pursuits of girls of her age became so vapid and inane, that she never engaged in them, and even shrank from companionship with her young friends; and Mrs. Holden saw, with alarm, that Emily was suffering mentally and physically, without being able to devise a remedy for her. It was this, which led her to accede more cheerfully to her departure from home. She thought a change might prove beneficial to her, and, therefore, without entering into any of Emily's magnificent plans for the future,

she consented to her entering on the weary-
ing life of a factory girl.

The next Monday morning, therefore,
witnessed Emily's departure to Lowell, as
different a place from the town of her nativity, as could well be imagined. Here she
found facilities for mental culture, beyond
what she had dreamed of possessing any
where outside the walls of a literary institution. Books, periodicals, and newspapers,
were all about her; circulating and Sabbath
school libraries were at her command; lec-
tures from able men were of weekly occurrence; and, in addition, she soon secured
the services of a teacher, to whom she went
nightly for instruction. By means of the
closest economy of time, she found much
leisure for mental cultivation. She allowed
herself no recreation; she curtailed the
hours of sleep, and applying herself assid-
uously, and learning almost intuitively, her
progress was astonishingly rapid. Even the
short half hour devoted to meals was abridg-
ed by her; and often, when some of her giddy companions returned home from a dance
or a party, near day-dawning, they would
find her absorbed in study, and bowed over
her books.

In this way she passed six months—laboring, during the day, to the very utmost of her ability, and studying, at night, with all the intensity of her soul—when, finding that the gains she had hoarded in a most miserly way were sufficient to carry her through two terms of a female seminary, at some little distance, of whose celebrity she had heard much during her factory life, she prepared to return home. The town of Lowell had proved a fortunate place to her. She had made extraordinary progress in self-culture, under the circumstances; had lost much of the rusticity, awkwardness and shyness of her manner; had won many friends, and had gained a full purse to assist her yet further in her praiseworthy exertions.

Overjoyed as were her mother and brother to fold their dear one to their hearts, they were painfully startled by her changed appearance. Her large eyes looked out from beneath her massive brow, darker and larger than ever—her pale cheeks were more colorless, and very thin. The application of the previous six months had been too intense—the spirit had worn away "its garment of flesh."

A few weeks were now given to recrea-

tion, and to the society of her mother and
brother, to whom she was incessantly pouring out the information she had acquired
during her absence. As the hungry devour
food, as the thirsty drink in water, so did
Henry sit at her feet, and devour every word
that fell from her lips. To him, she had become an oracle. She seemed completely
transformed; and when he gathered from
her lips the history of the past six months,
it strengthened his resolution to climb to
the very highest pinnacle of the hill of sci-
ence.

But again bidding adieu to her home,
Emily Holden entered the far-famed institution of learning — an event to which she had
long looked forward with eager anticipation.
The position she here took, on entering, was
by no means an inferior one. She found
herself superior to most of her age, great as
had been her disadvantages; and untiring,
devoted, enthusiastic student as she was, she
left her associates every day further in the
distance. Her fellow-students looked upon
her with wonder; they could not understand
the herculean efforts she was constantly making to comprehend fully, and to grasp surely,
every branch of study that came under her

observation.   To her teachers she was a
source of pride; they saw the glorious gifts
of the noble girl, her lofty aim, her enduring
purpose, her struggles for a high position in
the world of mind — they learned her history, they acquainted themselves with her
plans and wishes — and, struck with admiration of her hallowed ambition for herself and
brother, they offered her every advantage
the institution afforded, in its every department, for such service as she could consist-
ently afford them in teaching.

Here was a noble opportunity for her; and
so well was it improved, that a year had not
elapsed before she was one of the board of
instruction, with a full salary.   The trustees
of the institution foresaw that the duties of
teaching would not retard the progress of a
soul like hers, they were conscious that her
talents were of the most brilliant order; they
beheld the favorable impression she made
upon all who visited the institution, how
easily she won and retained the love of her
pupils, how apt she was to teach, how gentle
in governing; and from the sensation some
spirited little poems of hers had caused in
the world of letters, they anticipated for her,
if she chose it, a brilliant literary career.

They were, therefore, eager to secure her services, at even a high compensation.

And now a settled purpose was in her heart, though the desire that underlaid- it had existed there for years. She now resolved, at any and every sacrifice, to give her brother the means of a superior education. She instantly placed him in a preparatory school, though the expense of this would consume, per annum, three fourths of her salary. She knew that her brother's progress would draw more largely on her means; he could not pass through college for nothing; and she felt it imperative upon her to prepare for this exigency. Large offers from the southern section of our country had frequently been sent to teachers, in the institution with which she was connected. An acquaintance with music was an important desideratum in a teacher preparing for the south, and she now bent all her powerful energies to obtain this accomplishment, that she might be well prepared for the next lucrative situation that offered itself in that quarter. As usual, success crowned her efforts; and she had not been two years a teacher, when she stood at the head of a large and flourishing academy, in a southern

3

city. This increased income placed more ample means at her command, and Henry was enabled to pursue his studies without interruption.

Once, and once only, did she blench from the austere life she had imposed on herself.

In the immediate neighborhood of her residence, dwelt a wealthy and aristocratic family, whose especial *protegee* she became, immediately on her entrance into the town. Mr. and Mrs. Grey were not only people of wealth, style and fashion, but, incredible as it may seem, they were also kind and gentle-hearted, intelligent and thoughtful, and disposed to all the sweet charities of life. They were at first attracted towards Emily by the peculiar beauty of her pale, pensive face, and the sweetness of her manners; and afterwards they learned to love her for her noble self-forgetfulness, for her cultivated mind, and easy and elegant conversation.

Scarcely was she installed in their kind regards, when Walter, their only son, came home from college, on a visit. Having lived in almost monastic seclusion, while pursuing his studies, he had formed but few female acquaintances; and Emily, then in the perfection of her youthful beauty, burst upon him, like the vision of an houri. A second and third visit to his home became perilous to both; and having at last completed his studies, and received admittance to the bar, he returned home joyfully, to make arrangements for the practice of his profession in his native town.

Walter now sought Emily's society as studiously as she avoided his; and while the delicate and marked homage he paid her thrilled her inmost being with a wild delight, and infused into her soul a heaven of happiness, it yet caused her the most poignant sorrow, for she knew how hopeless was the affection he was cherishing, and how sad would be his awakening from the blissful dreams he was indulging. Moreover, she saw that, highly as his parents esteemed her, they had other views for their son than marriage with a governess; and that, while she rose daily in favor with one, she lost caste with the other. She, therefore, absented herself more and more from the mansion of the Greys, and wrapped around her, more and more closely, her maidenly reserve.

One evening, she was sitting alone, sad and weary. She had been thinking long and deeply and painfully. The conflict within,

3c

between love and duty, was not yet closed; and, for the first time, she murmured at her destiny.

Before this inward struggle was over, and while yet reasoning her rebellious heart to subjection, Walter Grey was with her. Despairing of meeting her accidentally, he had sought an interview, to declare his idolatrous affection, and, if possible, to win her who had become the light of his life. With a saddened heart, Emily listened to his avowal of love; but, though deeply moved, she gave a firm but gentle refusal to his proposals. It was in vain that he sat beside her, and urged his suit till the evening deepened into night. Although he drew from her the tearful confession that his love was returned, it availed him little; for, at the same moment, she withdrew her hand from his warm clasp, declaring that she had already chosen her lot, and should never marry.

It was impossible for him to penetrate to the reason that lay behind this resolution, or in the least to shake it. Emily, though moved to the very soul, was firm. The death of his hopes was also the destruction of her dream of happiness; and while she was putting out the light of his life, she was also involving herself in "darkness that could be felt"—and yet she was resolute, immovable. She feared her own weakness, and forbore to divulge her plans for her brother, the execution of which would require of her yet years of labor; nor did she allude to his parents' evident dislike of their son's preference—for she feared he might overcome these obstacles, which to her were, and, she thought, ought to be, insuperable.

"And so you have decided!" said Walter, rising to leave; "and you deliberately quench the dearest hope of my life, and turn back the only rill of happiness that flows for me!"

An expression of pain darted over Emily's features.

"You say that you love me, Emily; but how can I reconcile this assertion with your cruelty? Oh, Emily," he urged, passionately, "if you do indeed love me, take back your decision!"

"You know not what you ask," answered Emily, mournfully; "you know not what great interests are wrapped up in that decision."

"Emily," he said earnestly, "have you

thought that you will not always be vigorous
and young and self-sustained as now?"

She bowed, in assent.

"There will come days, by and by, when
health will fail, and friends be gone — when
your mother will slumber in the church-yard,
and your brother be so involved in the cares
of life, so entangled by new ties and affections, as to be dead to you. So will it be
with other friends. You alone, if you persist in your decision, will be without new
ties and friendships, to supply those that will
be lost to you. You will find yourself that
most desolate of all beings, a lonely woman,
verging into old age, without an eye to look
lovingly upon you, a voice to speak cheer-
ingly."

Emily wept.

"To whom, then, will you turn for comfort, or support? — who will buoy up your
sinking heart, and smooth your rugged
path?"

"Ah, Walter, have you forgotten there is
a God in heaven, who will never desert the
faithful and true?"

"No, Emily, but we need earthly friends;
and as life recedes, and death draws near,
we shall need sympathy and support — we

shall need the arms of love about us, the comforts of affection! Ah, Emily, it requires a brave heart to go through life alone — a strong heart! Have you thought of all these things?"

".Yes."

"And yet you accept this lonely lot as yours?"

"It is not mine to refuse it."

"You will not yield it, even for me?"

"I may not — I dare not!"

"You deceive yourself — you deceive me, Emily — you do not love me!"

A fresh burst of grief came from her heart, and she sobbed, "Forbear, forbear, Walter!"

He rose, and took her hand. "Forgive me," he said; "I am excited and wretched. I do you wrong. Ah, how desolate will life be now! — you will suffer — we must both be miserable — and why, I cannot understand. Farewell! — I shall see you no more. God bless you, Emily! God bless us both!" And wringing her hand wildly, he rushed from the room.

With a low cry of anguish, Emily reached out her arms as if to detain him, and then sank down upon the seat from which she had

risen, while the agony of her soul rolled over
her. How inexpressibly her heart yearned
after him, whose pleas for love she had refused; and how desolate, how reft of all
hope and light, loomed up before her the
years to come!

There are struggles which exhaust years
of life, and leave us almost callous to all
after trial. Of this nature was the struggle
through which Emily passed. Time, the
pressure of care and duty, and her own
strong mind and heart, eventually carried
her through this "Slough of Despond;" but
the vigor, enthusiasm, and elasticity of her
spirit were gone, and she had then a "heart
for any fate." She again moved on in the
discharge of duties, seeking happiness in the
resources of her mind and heart, in letters
from home, and in the improvement of her
pupils, to whom she was an object of affection and reverence.

Twelve years thus passed away, their
monotony only broken by one visit to her
early home, and widowed mother. By her
untiring efforts, she had raised the academy
over which she presided to the highest rank;
she had earned an enviable reputation as a
teacher, while her name was never men-

tioned but with encomiums by the magazine-reading public. Her ceaseless labor, and, more than all, the fiery ordeal through which she had passed, had wrought sad ravages on her physical being; and even those accustomed to her pale face and large dark eyes were at times startled by the ghastliness of her cheek, and the hollowness of the lustrous orbs that burned beneath her brow.

Meanwhile, Henry had graduated with the highest honors; and then, at his sister's earnest request, who represented herself abundantly able to furnish funds for an extensive and protracted tour, he traveled in Europe and the East, for two or three years. Appreciating the kindness of his sister, Henry was stirred to the depths of his soul with gratitude; and despatched to her, from every possible point of his tour, graphic sketches of all that interested him, making copious entries in his note-book, where he omitted or failed in letter-writing. Noble in person, glorious in mental endowment, rich in culture, improved by travel and communion with the world, he returned home, where the editorial duties of a periodical, long famous in the world of letters, were laid upon him, and soon afterwards he was elected to a professorship in a newly organized college, in one of the Western states.

Having achieved the dearest wish of her heart, and placed her brother in a position where his influence was widely felt, and where his cultivated powers had a legitimate sphere of action — having also secured to her mother possession of the little homestead which had passed out of her hands — Emily Holden's thoughts turned to her early home, and her fond and aged parent. She had struggled bravely with life, and her earnest spirit was repaid for its efforts, by the glorious consummation it had achieved. But her spirit now was weary, and sighed for repose. True to her self-sacrificing, unselfish nature, she thought of her distant mother, whose sun was declining, the sands of whose life were well-nigh spent; and continuing to seek her happiness in that of others, she despatched to her the following letter, unfolding her plans and hopes for the future:

"Give me joy, dear mother! for my days of exile are nearly accomplished, and my steps will soon be turned homeward. In a few days, I shall resign my charge here; and then, farewell to the land of birds and flowers and sunshine, and hence for bleak and rocky New England, the home of my heart.

I am coming home, dear mother, to do what I can to render the evening of your days pleasant. I have many a sweet anticipation of the happy hours I shall spend with you, in telling you of the past, in talking of the majestic genius of our dear Henry — God bless him! — whose motto is 'Excelsior!' and who is doing so much good in the world.

The days have been when *your* arm gave me support, when *your* hand guided me, when *your* powers were taxed for my amusement; but now, I am going to 'turn the tables,' and you shall be the supported, *I* the supporter — you the guided, *I* the leader. Together we will spend the long evenings, — you occupied with your knitting, I with my sewing, or in reading to you. You shall lean on my arm to church; you shall sit still and behold me engage in the domestic employments of my youth, which I have not wholly forgotten. Our little cottage shall be made to look cheery and cosy within, through the aid of light paint, paper, and scrupulous cleanliness; while without it, we will teach flowers to bloom, and birds to sing. Occasionally, Henry will come to us, in all the glory of his ripe and exalted manhood; and then heaven will come down to us, and we shall need no other happiness. Oh, mother, is it possible that I shall realize these sweet anticipations — that such summery days will come to me, when life seems now one long, unsunned winter? I have so long sojourned with strangers, that to throw my arm around my mother's neck, and to lean my head on her bosom — to hear her dear voice lovingly pronounce my name, and to see her dim eyes gazing fondly into my own — seems a bliss sweet beyond comparison. I have so long buffeted the storms of life and been lifted upon its waves, that to cast anchor in the quiet haven of home, seems as inviting as the rest of heaven. Oh, my Father, grant me the realization of these dreams, that bring delicious tears to my eyes, and a new sense of life to my heart!

I shall be with you, dear mother, shortly after this reaches you; till then, adieu! EMILY."

Resigning the post she had so long filled

with honor and satisfaction, Emily Holden now turned her face homewards.

It was near the close of an afternoon in the early fall, when the stage left her at the village inn, more than a mile from her mother's residence, which was in a retired part of the town. Declining the proffer of a carriage, and ordering her baggage sent after her, she started on foot towards home, anticipating, with trembling eagerness, the joyful surprise of her mother, on seeing her enter the cottage, unannounced by the rumbling of wheels. The road was one which she had often traveled in her girlhood, and she interested herself in noting the changes that had occurred during her absence. Suddenly she was aroused from her pleasing state of mind, by the heavy undulation of the church bell, that struck a knell for a funeral, or recent death.

As she reached the church, the tolling ceased, and, according to the custom of many of the remote and primitive villages of New England, the bell commenced "striking the age" of the deceased. Emily paused to count the strokes. The last stroke of the bell, at last, vibrated on the air — the age denoted was sixty years. Emily remembered that it was also her mother's age. She stood as if rooted to the ground, waiting for the bell to strike once more; — one stroke would signify that the deceased was a man, two that it was a woman. Solemnly, slowly, heavily, the strokes came — two of them. The blood receded from Emily's cheek, and went rushing back to her heart; but seeing the old sexton issue from the church door, which he locked behind him, and descend the steps, she summoned all her powers, and advanced towards him.

"Can you tell me, sir, who is dead?" she asked.

"Why, yes ma'am," replied the old man; "it's the widder Holden, that lives down there in the little white house yunder. She's been mighty poorly this long time; but we all hoped she would hold out till her darter got home from the Suth'ard, that she's been expectin' this great while — but the old lady died this mornin'."

Emily fell heavily to the ground. Astonished at the effect produced by his words, the old man took her in his arms to a neighboring house, where, after long efforts, she was restored to consciousness. "Carry me to my mother! Carry me to my mother!"

she said, like a sick child; and they took her
to the cottage, where lay the sheeted form
of her deceased parent. In tearless agony
Emily kissed the eyes, sealed in the sleep
that knows no waking and felt that the last
hold of her affections was torn away! Universal sympathy was felt for her, throughout
the town; but while others wept freely for
her, her eyes were glazed and dry; and
though all hearts and homes were opened to
her, she was firm in her determination to remain at the cottage. "I shall have another
home, shortly," she said, as if speaking pro-
phetically; "let me remain here, for the present."

As soon as the news of his mother's death,
and his sister's return, reached him, Henry
made preparations for the future residence
of the latter with himself. He was on the
eve of marriage with a fair girl, the counter-
part of the sister to whom he owed so much;
and he was resolved that the home of Emily
should henceforth be with them, and that she
should abandon the arduous profession at
which she had so faithfully labored.

He came immediately for her; but the little cottage was empty. Emily was not there;
she had rejoined the mother, whose declining

days she hoped to beautify, in that better world, where there is no sorrow. He was shown to her low grave in the churchyard, and the following note — her dying words to him — was placed in his hands:

"MY DEAR BROTHER:

Standing just on the verge of the valley of the shadow of death, I pause, for a moment, to bid you farewell. The world is now behind me, the grave at my feet, and heaven — HEAVEN — is full in view! Henry, I am dying! I shall never again see you with mortal vision; my summons hence has reached me, and I may not tarry till your arrival. Yet I am reconciled to the termination of my life, for I have accomplished all that was given me to do; I have fulfilled my mission; I am ready to go. I now seem to have no object in life. You do not need my further aid; our dear mother is translated to her rest — and worn, wearied, depressed, I accept with thankfulness the repose of the grave.

Do not mourn my departure — be not pained that you find me gone. Though invisible to you, I shall not be separated from you—not removed. You have been inexpressibly dear to me in life — you are in death — you will be in eternity. I shall be with you always, and with her whom you have taken to your heart; and you will both perceive my spiritual presence, though in bodily form you will see me no more.

And now, brother, friend of my soul, farewell! Remember the struggles of our early youth for emancipation of soul, and deal kindly with all similarly situated. God has lifted you up, by your great talents, above the mass of mankind; — consecrate them to his service.

Farewell! I am weary, and the rest of the churchyard, whose white stones I see gleaming in the distance, seems inviting and sweet. Farewell, dear, dear brother — farewell!   EMILY."

With a bursting heart, Henry went out to the grave of her to whom he owed all that he was; and there, where only God beheld him, he consecrated himself anew to good-. ness and truth. Kneeling on the grassy turf, beneath which slumbered his mother and sister, he called on her who had given him birth, and on her whose heart and life had been stepping-stones to his present exaltation, to witness the vow that he made to be the champion of right and virtue — a vow which his after life fulfilled — a vow that never was broken.

THE SALE OF THE HOMESTEAD.

Six years had passed away since the sleep of death had weighed down the eyelids of Mr. Howard, and his last resting-place had been hollowed beneath the cypress and the willow. Many and various changes had occurred during that time, and the great sorrow that had been sent into his family by his death, had been deepened and darkened by other succeeding reverses and disasters. The large and valuable estate, which at his decease, was not wholly unencumbered, had become more heavily embarrassed through bad management, until heavy mortgages nearly covered its whole value. Amiable, confiding and credulous, reared in affluence, destitute of any financiering ability, without practical knowledge of the world, and devoid of the energy most needful to her in her circumstances, Mrs. Howard trusted to dishonest agents, and rapacious money-seekers, who hesitated not to defraud her of the por-

4

tion left to her and her fatherless children, and who, in the short space of half a dozen years, reduced her thousands to a mere pittance.

Then, too, sickness had been busy in the household, and death had claimed two of the fairest and most precious blossoms of the family tree—the eldest two of the family, both sons, the mother's pride and dependence, who, with tears and heart-breaking sorrow were laid to rest, in the private burial ground on the estate, beside their lamented father. The anger of Mrs. Howard's family, which had been excited by her husband shortly after their marriage, by some business transaction which clashed with the interests of his wealthy and somewhat tyrannous father-in-law, burned as fiercely as ever against her, during her sad and troubled widowhood, when more than ever she prayed that it might be averted.

But sadder than all other changes was that observed in their mother, by the dutiful and loving children, who clung to the timid, shrinking widow with more than idolatrous affection. Each succeeding year she had drooped under the pressure of care, trouble and sorrow, that laid their heavy burdens

upon her, becoming paler, thinner, and sadder, until it seemed as if even the transforming process of death could not farther etherealize her. Physical debility at first only
confined her to her room, which the watchful
love of her children rendered a most pleasant
retreat; but soon she was compelled to keep
her bed most of each day, and then imperceptibly such weakness stole over her, that
it became necessary to lift her from her bed
to her arm-chair, and back from the arm-
chair to the bed, like a mere babe. Still all
the while she cherished delusive hopes of
recovery, and even when the thought of
death stole pleasantly over her, as the
thought of night comes to the worn and
weary laborer, for her children's sake she
put away the vision, and predicted that "she
should be better by and by." Now she was
sure that the breath of spring would revive
her, and then that the bracing air of winter
would recuperate her wasting energies; but
all the while she failed, and faded, and sunk
into the grave, till all but those who loved
her most, and prayed most earnestly for her
life, saw that there was but a step between
her and death.

The last earthly spring had budded for

4D

her, and there was no longer room for hope. The spiritual vision of the wasting invalid became enlarged, and she saw earth receding from her view, and heaven opening to her; while the stricken children, who would fain have accompanied their beloved mother through the dark valley, saw that she was passing from their embrace. It was not possible for either party to deceive itself longer —Mrs. Howard was dying. She summoned her children to her bedside, a sorrowing, helpless group, the eldest just emerging from childhood, the youngest, a child of seven summers. All her anxieties for them were at an end; she had done with the world and its cares; and though she could not see the way, she was sure the All-wise Father would provide for them and have them in his keeping. She enjoined on them another appeal to their wealthy, but relentless grand-parent, adjured them to hold fast their integrity, and then, with words of benediction on her dying lips, with love beaming from her dim eyes, and hope shining like a halo from her pale brow, she bade them "good-by," and taking the hand of the Savior, walked firmly and fearlessly through the dark valley of the shadow of death. And now was the world dark indeed to the orphaned brothers and sisters; the love which had lighted their way had gone out in death, and timid, wretched and alone, they clung to one another in sorrowing helplessness. 'The waters of affliction which before had only dashed around their feet, had now swelled breast high, and it seemed as if they would be borne to despair by them : it was impossible for them to be comforted.

But despite all grief and sorrow, the tide of business and worldly affairs rolls on as ever, and the routine of every-day life is but slightly disturbed. The funeral rites were scarcely over, and Mrs. Howard laid at rest beside her husband and children, before Ellen, the eldest of the family, not yet seventeen, found forced upon her the necessity of planning and thinking for the dreary future before her. What was to be done? She knew not, and in her ignorance consulted the kind-hearted and sympathizing people who came to offer their condolence to the afflicted household. Every variety of advice and counsel was given her, and Ellen found herself bewildered, rather than aided. But the opinion which obtained most widely among her advisers was, that the estate had

better be sold, and also all the personal property not necessary to them, and the debts of
the family liquidated, when it was hoped a
sum would be left sufficient to maintain them
until means for their farther support could be
devised. It was said that Ellen could support herself by teaching; Fanny, the next
eldest, who displayed remarkable taste, might
be apprenticed to a milliner; Henry and
Granville should both be bound to some
artisan, till they had acquired a trade; while
very many in town were willing to take
Susie and Clara, the youngest, and the pet
lambs of the household, and adopting them
into their families, rear them as their own
children.

But from all this Ellen shrank with terrible reluctance. What! sell the dear homestead, where her brothers and sisters, with
herself, had first seen the light of day, where
their infancy and childhood had been passed,
where lay her parents and four of their children! Should she sell the graves of these
dear ones, their last resting-place! No,
never! never! She would never consent to
it: they would practice the most rigid economy, they would endure privations and the
most pinching poverty, they would labor like

Helots, but sell the homestead they could not, must not, would not.

Nor did the other advice find more favor with her. What would their mother say to see her darling children scattered hither and thither, some drudging at trades, when they should be conning lessons, and others forced to be kitchen menials, ere they were out of their babyhood? No, she could not consent to this; she was the eldest, and appointed by nature and Providence to be the guardians of the orphaned children, and how could she expect the blessing of her sainted parents would rest upon her, if she permitted such cruel dismemberment of the family! And poor Ellen was as much at a loss as ever to know what to do. All felt for her, but none were able to give her better advice than that which she had refused to follow; and though friends still clustered around her, friends in outward seeming, if not in reality, who were continually proffering their varying advice, she lingered and hesitated, and inefficient, as her mother had been before her, did nothing.

But the necessity from which she shrank, was at last forced upon her; and her irresolution was changed by compulsion into spas-

modic action. The legal adviser, who had
transacted business for her mother, waited
upon her, while she was in this undecided
state, and informed her that two or three of
the heaviest mortgages had been foreclosed
by those who held them, and as it was now
too late to redeem them, and she had not the
means, it would be necessary to sell the
estate. This intelligence came like a thun-
der-bolt upon poor Ellen. She knew too
little of business matters to anticipate or
expect the occurrence of which he informed
her; and it came, therefore, with overpower-
ing force upon her. There was now no way
but to let matters take their own course.
With the loss of the estate they would lose
their home: they had no relatives in that
section of the country; of their father's kindred they knew nothing, and their maternal
relatives they had reason to believe would
be hostile to them, so that they would be
forced to dispose of all the personal property, with the exception of some valuable
and portable articles, which it was deemed
advisable they should retain. The heart of
Ellen died within her. This seemed the
crowning calamity of her life, and the future
was now invested with additional terror.

Dispersion, degradation, and little less than beggary seemed before her. With a heart like lead in her bosom, she gathered her brothers and sisters around her, and imparted to them the knowledge of this fresh affliction, and while she intended to give them an example of fortitude and self-reliance, in her own demeanor, she only abandoned herself to the most overwhelming grief. It was sad tidings for them all; and as they realized that the hour was approaching, which would deprive them of their home, and would rend them from each other, they clung to one another more fondly, and wept more inconsolably.

But in the depth of this utter darkness, Ellen, feeble, ignorant, shrinking and inefficient, yet saw light. Earth seemed pitiless to them; fortune had frowned upon them; but God was yet left them, their mother's God, before whom they had bowed with her each night and morning; and to Him they now appealed in their hour of extremity. Kneeling together in the sanctuary of that consecrated room where their mother had died, the desolate children joined in the broken, but earnest prayer that came from Ellen's lips and full heart, and when they

rose from their supplication, if they saw their
way no clearer, their hearts were yet calmer,
their spirits lighter. And now Ellen be-
thought her of her mother's dying injunction, and dismissing the younger children to
their slumbers, and asking the aid of the
elder ones, she sat down and wrote her
grandfather the following simple epistle:.

"MR. THOS. BARTON:

"Dear Sir,—In obedience to the dying injunction
of my departed mother, I take the liberty of addressing you, her father, whom I have never known but
through her conversation. Three months ago, she
left earth for a happier home, and by her death six
of us are rendered desolate and destitute orphans.
Ignorant of the world, friendless, disconsolate and in
poverty, we know not what to do. Our father's
large estate is advertised to be sold at auction, to
pay off the heavy mortgage upon it, and what little
personal property we possess must be sacrificed to
liquidate other debts. We shall then be afloat upon
the world, utterly penniless. . The eldest of us is
nearly seventeen, the youngest nearly eight years
old. We are all willing to work and aid ourselves,
but we need direction and advice. We desire above
all things not to be far separated from each other, as
when we have lost our home, the dear homestead
where we were born, where sleep our parents, and
four of our brothers and sisters, the society of each
other will be the only happiness we shall know.

"In this sad state of things, to whom is it more
natural for us to apply than to the father of our
sainted mother—that father on whose head she sup-
plicated blessings even with her latest breath — that
father whom she ever loved, and taught her children
to revere and to pray for? I am aware, dear Sir, of
the unhappy state of feeling that has existed between

the two families — but oh, forgive the offence of our
father against you! He has long slept beneath the
clods of the valley, and now our dear, *dear* mother
has joined him! Can you not then forgive them,
and look compassionately on their children, who
have never injured you, no, not in thought? We
beseech you, by the memory of that glorified spirit,
whose ascension to heaven we so deeply deplore, by
the memory of the dear Redeemer, who forgave his
deadliest enemies even on the cross, by the love of
that God in whom we still trust in all our darkness,
forgive our parents, extend to us reconciliation and
pardon, and bestow on us your affection, your sympathy, your counsel and aid. God will reward you
for it, and my mother in her glorious home above
will shower upon you silent, but not unperceived
blessings for it.

     "With respect and affection,
      "ELLEN HOWARD."

"There," said Ellen, folding the sheet, "I
have done as mother commanded; but I am
sure my letter will go on a bootless errand.
We shall never hear from it, I fear."

"No," sighed Fanny disconsolately, leaning her head on her hand with an air of
dejection, "if it were not that mother re-
quested it, I should laugh, wretched as we
are, at the idea of applying to grandfather.
If he would not reply to *her* letters, written
after father's death, he will not to *ours*."

"Well, now, I have more faith than either
of you," said Henry, a remarkably serene,
spiritual and intellectual lad; "it seems to

me that letter *will* be answered, sister Ellen, and favorably too."

"Heaven grant you may be a true prophet!" and Ellen kissed his calm, white brow; "but it is so many years since grandfather began to cherish anger against our parents, that I have little hope from that quarter, I confess."

The next morning, with a trembling but hopeful heart, Henry committed the letter to the post-office, and then, patiently as they could, they awaited the result of its mission. Weeks wore away; everywhere notices of the approaching sale of their home met their eyes, the house and grounds were ransacked by intended purchasers, questions which they deemed impertinent, and shrank from answering, were continually asked them, and as continually were they urged to make some arrangements about the future; but they hoped, vaguely and faintly to be sure, that their grandfather, or some one of their relatives might yet appear for their relief. But though Henry made his appearance at the office on each arrival of the mail, no letter came in reply to the one Ellen had despatched. The faint hope which had lighted the heart of the Howards died completely

away, and when on the day before the auction, Henry returned from the office empty-
handed as ever, they said to one another in
bitter despondence, "We must now make up
our minds to see our dear home pass into
the hands of strangers; there is no other
alternative."

When the sun went down that evening,
hand in hand they took their last walk
around the dear premises, and now mutely,
and now with broken words and flowing
tears, bid the scenes and haunts of their
childhood farewell. They walked through
the green meadow, in whose meandering
stream they had bathed their weary feet in
the busy and happy season of haymaking;
they passed through the orchard, where
showers of fragrant blossoms had rained on
them in the spring, and where, with shout
and glee, their tiny hands had helped to har-
vest the rosy and golden stores of autumn.
Then they stopped to look their last on the
grape-vine bowers, to rest for a few moments
on the circular seat with which their father
had girdled the graceful old elm, to peep
into the stables, carriage-house, dove-cotes,
and the Gothic dwelling of Lion, the house-
dog, who accompanied them in this last ram-

ble about their old homestead, and then they
turned into the garden. But here the smoth-
ered grief of their hearts burst forth irre-
pressibly. Here were the honey-suckles
their mother had trained, the rose-bushes
she had planted, the jessamine she had trel-
lised, the flower-beds she had laid out, the
walks she had designed, the shrubs she had
nurtured — nowhere could they turn their
eyes, but they were reminded of her who
was all to them, of her whose loss to them
was irreparable. The sense of their bereave-
ment, that time had somewhat deadened,
became fresh as if it had occurred yesterday,
and they wept in one another's embrace, like
orphaned children indeed.

Long they lingered in the tasteful enclo-
sure, and not till the purple twilight had
deepened into evening, did they pass to the
most sacred and touching spot of all—the
family burial-ground. Awed and saddened,
they passed under the black shade of the
cypress and willow, that sighed mournfully
in the evening air, and sat down beside the
little mounds, whose marble slabs, gleaming
in the dim light, bore the names of the calm
sleepers beneath. Here bloomed roses and
pansies, the amaranth and heliotrope, planted

by the surviving children, who sought to
beautify the place, and to express by flowery
emblems the love and hope of their hearts
for the departed. Tearfully they sought to
comfort one another, expressing hopes they
did not cherish, and expectations which had
no place in their hearts, and not until the
dampness of the dews warned them of their
protracted stay, did they seek the house, to
await with heavy hearts the advent of the
next terrible day—the day of the dreaded
auction.

Among the many individuals who had visited the house and grounds of the Howards
since it had been advertised for sale, was
one person towards whom the orphans felt
a strong repugnance. The object of their
dislike was tall and gaunt, with a shrewd
and sinister cast of face, obstinate, reserved,
and prying, who succeeded in getting at the
intentions and purposes of others marvelous-
ly, while he would have puzzled the most
skilful inquisitor with his vague and ambigu-
ous replies. With an insolent and independ-
ent air, he stalked through the various apart-
ments of the mansion, giving utterance to
remarks that indicated great lack of refine-
ment, and catechising the children concern-

ing their prospects and the causes of their embarrassment, until their gentle spirits rebelled, and they gave their rude visitor to understand that they deemed his queries insolent. To increase still more the abhorrence of the young Hówards, he brushed Tabby, the tortoise-shell kitten from his knee, upon which she had purringly jumped, as if the petted favorite had been a venomous reptile; Lion, their tawny playfellow, received a kick from him, as he lay sunning himself in the door-way, which roused the animal into an attitude of defence and indignation, that startled the impassive and stolid Mr. Jenkins. As he perambulated the garden, his large and heavy feet, instead of keeping within the limits of the graveled walks, trod here upon the box borders, and there into the very heart of a flower-bed; now he plucked the crowning blossoms of a rare exotic, and then, in gathering a flower, drew the whole plant from the earth; while to complete the list of his offences, he pulled Henry slyly by the ear, as if he were a mere roguish boy, instead of a dignified youth, chucked Clara and Susie under the chin, as they were packing their baby-houses, and asked Ellen when she thought of moving, and where. As he completed his survey of the premises, and announced his intention to purchase the estate, a simultaneous outcry burst from the younger children, who expressed the hope that he might not be successful in his plans,—a wish that he heard with a sardonic countenance, when he turned and left them to themselves.

The day of the sale dawned, bright, fair, and balmy, although the children had fervently hoped it might prove stormy and blustering. At an early hour, crowds of people thronged to the Howard estate, many desiring to effect some purchase, many as idle lookers-on, and some few to comfort and sustain the homeless and penniless orphans in their trial. Earliest and most prominent among the multitude, appeared the obnoxious Mr. Jenkins, who, with the familiarity of an old acquaintance, accosted the distressed family, passing the usual compliments of the day, and congratulating them on the favorable prospect there appeared for an advantageous sale.

The personal property was first disposed of; and to the infinite annoyance of the young Howards, and the utter astonishment of the gazers-on, every thing valuable, every

thing that it would be impossible for them
to replace, every thing they hoped would be
purchased by their neighbors and townspeo-
ple, passed into the hands of the detested
Jenkins. The beautiful and costly furniture
of the parlors, rare pictures and all—Mr.
Howard's library, his cabinet of curiosities,
his busts, philosophical apparatus, and even
his gold watch—the coach, carriage-horses,
and Henry's black pony—in short, every
thing they had hoped to see pass into other
hands, was coolly bidden off by him, who
ran up the prices of articles against his com-
petitors, as if the gold of California were at
his command.

At last, the auctioneer announced the sale
of the estate. At this notice, the excited
multitude gathered around him, few of whom
cared to bid on so heavy property. There
was one individual, however, anxious to secure it—an old resident of the town, wealthy,
popular, and friendly to the family whose
fallen fortunes had caused the auction. It
was also known that Jenkins was desirous to
buy the estate, though few present doubted not
but he would be overbidden by his wealthy
rival. There were forty acres in the whole
property, and it was to be sold undivided.

The auction commenced. The first bid was made by Mr. Wilson, the townsman of the Howards, who offered fifty dollars per acre for the entire lands. This was promptly responded to by Jenkins, who advanced ten dollars on the bid of his rival, and a brisk competition ensued between them, until one hundred and twenty-five dollars had been offered by Jenkins. The scene now became a most exciting one. The dense crowd had pressed nearer and nearer to the auctioneer's stand, until the two rivals were closely hemmed in by a compact wall of human beings, few of whom did not desire that Jenkins might be defeated in his plans of buying. Mr. Wilson was highly excited. His face was pale, his eyes flashing with a lightning glance, his lips parted, while his movements betokened great nervous agitation. On the other hand, Jenkins was impertubably calm and collected. With his hat partly slouched over his eyes, with an impassive and sardonic face, he was whittling away as coolly as though he felt no interest whatever in the proceedings about him.

"One hundred fifty dollars!" bid Wilson, while the crowd around gasped for breath.

"One hundred fifty dollars is offered for the estate!" shouted the auctioneer; "one hundred fifty dollars! who bids more? going at one hundred fifty—going"—

"One hundred fifty-five!" drawled Jenkins, without raising his eyes, or ceasing to whittle.

"One hundred fifty-five dollars per acre is offered! the land worth every cent of it! Am I offered more? One hundred fifty-five! one hundred fifty-five! going—who bids—going"—

"One hundred sixty!" shrieked Wilson, in a tone of exasperation, casting dagger-like glances at his *nonchalant* competitor.

"One hundred sixty is offered! who bids higher than one hundred and sixty? Who bids? who bids? going at one hundred and sixty—going"—

"One hundred sixty-five!" offered Jenkins, with the utmost *sang froid*.

"The bid is raised to one hundred sixty-five dollars! does any one offer more? going at one hundred sixty-five dollars, going"—

"One hundred seventy!" bid Wilson, while large beads of sweat stood on his forehead, and his face became deathly pale; at the same time dropping his head, and retreating

back a step or two into the crowd, with a
manner that said, "I shall go no higher!"

"I am offered one hundred seventy dollars
for this estate!" continued the auctioneer;
"who bids more—who bids? who bids?
going—going"—

"One hundred and seventy-five!" continued Jenkins, as quite and cool as heretofore.

"One hundred seventy-five dollars? does
any one bid more? One hundred seventy-
five—one hundred seventy-five—going—
going—GONE!"—and the fall of his hammer
closed the contest. A murmur of disappointment ran through the crowd, when Jenkins
was announced as the purchaser, while all
now gathered round him, to ascertain his
intentions relative to the property. But he
was impenetrable; and though their queries
were most perseveringly pushed, they were
so cunningly evaded, or ambiguously answered, that with a muttered curse on the singular being, he was soon left to himself.

As for the Howards, their grief and cha-
grin were excessive; they had hoped a different fate for their beautiful home, and
could hardly be reconciled to the ill luck
that had given it to so repulsive a purchaser.
They found many to sympathize in their re-

gret at the termination of the sale, and temporary homes were freely offered them, until
they could make some arrangements for the
future. Mr. Jenkins also sought them out,
to inform them, in his unpleasant nasal
twang, that he would call in the evening,
and talk with them about the time when he
should expect them to give him possession
of his domains, at the same time assuring
them he was in no haste, and advising them
to make no hurried arrangements about moving — a piece of kindness which they could
hardly bring themselves to thank him for.

Gradually the crowds dispersed, stillness
settled upon the household, evening came,
and found them gathered in the usual sitting-
room — plunged in deeper dejection than
ever. The dwelling did not seem much dis-
mantled, for Mr. Jenkins had bid in nearly
every thing of value, and but little change
was visible in the interior of the house. But
it would have been pleasanter to the orphans,
had the choice treasures of the mansion been
scattered among the people of their acquaintance; it would have seemed less like sacrilege
than to have had them retained by this un-
couth, unrefined specimen of the human race.

"Only think of it!" said Henry; "all father's books are going to that booby, who, I dare say, can hardly read."

"What under the sun he wants of a library, I can't see!" continued Fanny; "or of such elegant furniture as that in the parlor."

"He has a family, I suppose," said Ellen, "and perhaps means to bring them here to live; that is my opinion, formed from the manner and kind of his purchases."

"Oh dear!" groaned Fanny; "I hope we shall move miles from here then, for I should die to see such coarse and vulgar people enjoying the conveniences and luxuries purchased by our parents."

"Hush, hush, sister!" mildly reproved Ellen; "it matters after all but little who has bought here, since we were obliged to sell. We ought to be thankful the property has sold so advantageously as it has."

"Ah me!" replied Fanny; "but only think how different it would have been, if our dear father had lived!"

"Oh well, Fanny dear," was Ellen's soothing reply, who was just ready herself to burst into tears; "don't let's cherish sad thoughts; heaven will provide for us in some way!"

"Yes, Ellen, I think we shall be cared

for!" added Henry; "and I have not yet given up all hope of grandfather."

A bitter and almost mocking smile flitted across the faces of the sisters, but before they could reply, a loud knock was heard at the hall door.

"It is Mr. Jenkins, again!" said Henry, while an expression of aversion passed over the faces of the whole family; and taking a lamp, he went to answer the summons. But instead of beholding the lank figure of Mr. Jenkins, when he opened the door, he saw a dignified and venerable old man, with silvery hair, who inquired for Ellen Howard. A thrill of joy ran through Henry's heart, as he invited the stranger to enter, and it was with the utmost difficulty he could command his steps so as to keep pace with the slow and measured tread of the new comer, as he showed him to the sitting-room. The old man paused a moment on the threshold of the room, and surveyed the interesting group seated within, with evident emotion.

"This is Miss Ellen Howard, for whom you inquired, Sir," said Henry, advancing towards his sister.

Ellen rose to receive her guest, while the old gentleman extended his hand, and grasping hers warmly, looked earnestly in her face, but still without uttering a word. He was evidently trying to master some strong emotion within, that nearly overpowered him. But Henry could keep silence no longer. His convictions had grown stronger every moment, until now they amounted almost to certainty. With a kindling eye, and a glowing cheek, he seized the stranger's hand, and burst forth with the impassioned inquiry— "Are you not, Sir, Mr. Barton, the father of my mother, and consequently my grandfather ?"

The question brought fire into all eyes, and color into all cheeks. In an instant the little group were on their feet, and the old gentleman was surrounded. "Are you our grandfather ?" "Oh, tell us, Sir, are you our mother's father ?" "Are you indeed our grandfather ?" were the queries launched at him in the same breath, by all the children, and with the utmost eagerness.

"Well, well !" said the old gentleman, with affected *brusquerie* of manner, starting back a little; "this is a pretty way to treat a stranger, and a grey-headed old man, too ! I don't know as I shall want to own such a wild set as grandchildren, but I suppose I shall be obliged to, if you are the children of Henry and Fanny Howard."

And now what a wild burst of joy there was! What jumping, and laughing, and shouting for gladness! What clapping of hands, and essaying of hurrahs! What triumphant reference to Henry's fulfilled predictions! What grateful exclamations, and rapturous embraces! All but Ellen seemed mad with delight; and she, poor thing! partly from the sudden revulsion of feeling, partly because it was her only way of expressing her deepest emotions, and partly because strongly reminded of her mother, sunk down and wept. Away flew the youngsters to their mother's room; the large armchair that had been undisturbed since her death, was wheeled out, and then, invited by five noisy tongues, and aided by five pairs of willing hands, Mr. Barton was seated in their very midst.

"But what are you crying for, Ellen?" he asked, dashing away a tear himself; "what are you crying for, child? are you sorry to see your old grandfather, who has taken a journey of six hundred miles at your request?"

"Sorry, grandfather? sorry?" answered

Ellen, "how can you think so? but oh, if our poor mother had lived to see this day!"

"Yes," said Fanny, "if mother could only know of our happiness! if she could only have seen you before she died, she would have closed her eyes more peacefully."

"Mother *does* know of our happiness," said Henry; "I have no doubt but from heaven she is looking on us now!"

"That's right, my boy!" said Mr. Barton, as with moist eyes, he looked on the noble youth; "that's right! always look on the bright side; let's seek to be happy to night. And now, how are your affairs? How is it about the estate? When does the sale of it come off?"

"Oh, it is sold, grandfather, it was sold to-day;" they all cried in a pitiful tone.

"Sold to-day! who bought it?"

"A horrid Mr. Jenkins, who bought every thing of any value."

"Ah, indeed!"

"He overbid everybody on the estate, and ran it up to seven thousand dollars."

"Seven thousand dollars! Whew! A pretty round sum for a farm like this!"

"He bought father's library, and all the parlor furniture, and the horses, too!"

"He did! Well, well! I should think he did pretty well!"

"Was 'nt it too bad, grandfather?"

"Well, I don't know as it was."

"Don't you wish you had got here earlier —just a day earlier?"

"Well, I don't know as I do;" and Mr. Barton seemed very much inclined to laugh.

"Why, grandfather? *We* are very sorry the estate went in the way it did!"

"It could not have been better disposed of," was the singular reply. The Howards were astonished; they knew not what to think of all this. But at this moment another knock was heard at the door, and Henry ushered in the "horrid Mr. Jenkins," amid the stifled exclamations, "A disagreeable fellow!" "I wish he'd keep away to-night!" "Send him off quick, sister Ellen!" But what was their astonishment to see the object of their dislike advance towards Mr. Barton with a look of recognition, and a low bow, which the latter acknowledged by a hearty shake of the hand.

"When did you arrive, Mr. Barton?" asked Mr. Jenkins, respectfully.

"Not an hour ago," replied Mr. Barton; "and thinking I might find you here, I came straight to the house. I have already learned how well you executed your commission; these youngsters have been telling me how fortunate you were."

"Yes, Sir," replied Jenkins; "I have succeeded not only in getting you the estate, but all the valuable property besides."

And now there was another outburst of astonishment. "*You*, grandfather! is the estate *yours?*" they asked incredulously.

"I expect it is," he replied, with laughter, "if Jenkins, my agent here, tells the truth."

"Why, grandfather, is it *really* yours?"

"You little unbelievers! yes, it is *really* mine."

"And shan't we have to move from it?"

"Not without you prefer it."

"And won't the furniture be carried away?"

"Not a splinter of it, if you want it to remain."

If there had been gladness before, there was ecstacy now; if their hearts had been full before, they overflowed now. Susie and Clara climbed into his lap, and almost suffocated him with kisses; Fanny and Ellen fell on the old man's neck, and wept, and sobbed, and laughed, while Mr. Barton himself cried and laughed like a girl. Henry and

Granville took Mr. Jenkins by the hand, "horrid" and "disagreeable" no longer, and thanked him a thousand times, and asked his forgiveness, and leading him to the sofa, bade him be seated among them.

"I reckoned you wouldn't feel so hard towards me when you come to know the rights of the case!" said the almost unmanned agent.

"There now, children," said Mr. Barton; "there now," rising and putting the children from him, "you are making a woman of me! Poor things, I did'nt know as you cared so much about your home."

But it was long before calmness was restored to the household. They had suffered so long and so keenly, their way had seemed so dark and hedged up, such despair had settled upon them, that now a reversion of their fortunes had taken place, their hearts were too full of joy, their bosoms too much charged with gratitude, to allow them to settle down into quietude in a moment. Mr. Jenkins soon took his leave, and then, till a late hour the happy children sat with their aged relative, talking of the past, planning for the future. The events of the last six years were unfolded to him with all their

variety of light and shade, and his tears mingled with theirs as he learned that their mother's letters, written after their father's death,
had never reached him; for it was pleasanter to believe the post had miscarried, than
that a father had been so vindictive towards
a being gentle and tender as their mother. .

And now had commenced the beginning
of better days to the young Howards. In a
few days, masons, carpenters, painters and
other artisans were employed by Mr. Barton,
who never did things by halves; thorough
repairs were made, a large and handsome
addition was erected, to enlarge the already
spacious mansion, and when he returned to
his distant home, there came to reside with
the orphans, a younger brother of their
mother's, with his wife and children, whose
business it was to manage the estate. The
sunshine of prosperity again beamed on
them; the studies of the younger children
were again resumed, their long-tried hearts
were solaced by the love of their new-found
kindred, and throughout their after lives
they had reason to look back upon the day
when occurred the sale of the homestead,—
an event which seemed to them at the time
only fraught with unmixed misery,—as one
of the most fortunate days of their lives.

THE HOUSE OF REST.

" Parva domus, sed magna quies."

Where ends the rugged steep of life,
   And pilgrims stay their bleeding feet,
Ere on to heaven they wend their way,
   A house of rest the travelers meet.

Forever is prepared its couch—
   Forever open stands its door;
And so alluring is its rest,
   The traveler turneth back no more.

Though small the house, a narrow home,
   Yet wondrous large is the respose;
And pilgrims, bowed with many a care,
   Here find a Lethe for their woes.

God hath built up this house of rest,
   And bid kind Death a vigil keep,
To lead his weary children in,
   And seal their eyes in dreamless sleep.

And angels wait without the door,
   To link with theirs a hand of love,
To lead them to a sunnier land,
   Where fraught with bliss the hours will move

THE SEWING SOCIETY.

"Come, now, Cousin Henry, *do* give me
your name for our sewing society; wont
you?" said Julia Bradley, coaxingly; and
laying her needle-work down in her lap, she
tossed back a shower of curls that had fallen
over her bright face, rested her elbow on the
arm of the sofa, leaned her chin on the palm
of her small hand, and fixed her merry, fun
loving eyes full on the sedate face of her
cousin.

"Pray, Julia, *do n't* teaze me any more
about that odious society," was the impatient
reply of Henry Marston, who hardly deigned
to raise his eyes from the paper he was reading; "I've told you, at least a dozen times,
that I do not wish to join it; then why urge
me farther?"

"Because, my sedate cousin, I have resolved to win you for one of our honorable
and honorary members — and it is a matter
of conscience with me, never to give up any-

6

thing upon which I have *resolved*. Can't
you afford the fifty cents' admission fee? If
not, why just say so, and in five minutes I'll
have a subscription paper started, headed by
myself, with the munificent donation of half
a dime.

"Thank you, Julia," said Henry, still poring over his newspaper; "but I think I
could raise the required fifty cents, unaided,
were I ambitious of joining you."

"Then why do you persist in declining my
invitation? Come, do lay away that old
musty paper, and answer me!" and the merry girl seized the journal yet moist from the
printing press, and laid it beside her on the
sofa. "Now, Mr. Sedateness, please tell me
why you refuse to join our society, and to
associate with us, evenings, as other young
gentlemen do."

"Let me answer your question in true
Yankee style, by asking another. Of what
benefit is your society? What good has it
ever accomplished? I know of a deal of
mischief that it has done, but I have yet to
learn that it has accomplished any good."

"*Mischief!*" and Julia's red lips pouted a
little. "Mischief, sir! What mischief has
it caused? I have never known any."

"Only think how much of the current gossip of the town has its origin in that society. Why, even you, Julia, complain of the scandal-propagating propensities of some of its members."

"La! is that all you mean?"

"Then add to this the offence that has been given to some of our best people, by your wild way of passing the evenings — in playing backgammon, chess, checkers, and whist, in singing silly love ditties, in dancing and similar amusements — and remember how much ill feeling this has engendered between the older and younger members; ill-feeling that, in some instances, has grown into positive hatred, and occasioned a war of words, if nothing worse."

"Don't make a mountain out of a molehill, Henry. But very few of our number have become disaffected, and though I confess we have been wild sometimes, yet it ought to be remembered that we are young, in the very heyday of life."

"Well, tell me of some good that the society has accomplished, that will counterbalance even this reduced evil."

"There is little that we *can* do — there is no opportunity for us to be useful in this

village.   Our church is completed, and hand-
somely furnished, and is all paid for; our
society is free from debt, our library well
stocked; so that really, there is little or nothing for us to do."

"*Nothing for you to do!*" and Henry's
face grew earnest in its expression, and he
spoke sternly.   "Look at widow Foster, in
the lane, who has seven children, all save the
eldest looking to her for support.   Think
how much you might cheer that lone, struggling woman, by meeting an afternoon at her
humble home, carrying your own provisions
for supper, and such donations as you could
afford, all of you during the afternoon sewing
for herself and fatherless children."

"But I do n't think Mrs. Foster would like
such an arrangement.   People say she is
very proud-spirited."

"I know her better than that; she is not
proud-spirited.   Then there is poor old Mrs.
Howard, whose children are dead, and who
lives alone, under the hill; would not a present of warm clothing, for this coming winter,
be acceptable, and would she not bless you
for remembering her?"

"Dear me! Henry, you ought to be chosen
one of the selectmen; for I verily believe

you know more about the town's poor than any one else."

"I *do* know this, Julia, that there are in this thriving village, individuals suffering from such poverty and distress as only God knows — and I do also know, that this sewing society, which you urge me to join, and which does nothing but gossip, drink tea, and flirt away the blessed evenings, might relieve a large portion of it, if it would."

"But you would not have us take the business of the town out of the hands of the selectmen, I hope. If you are going to make this a condition on which you will join us, I think Doomsday will find you still out of our circle."

"And I am certainly willing that it should, unless the character of the society be somewhat changed, and it assume a more useful aspect. Then, and not till then, shall I be willing to give you my name."

"And so I am to consider it decided, my utilitarian cousin! Well, it is all for the best that you should not join us, probably, for I am sure nobody but myself could ever bide your interminable preachments. Let me tell you, cousin Henry, that you are predestined, predetermined and foreordained to be a rusty, crusty, fusty old bachelor, and from the bottom of my heart I pity the woman that ever persuades you to be anything else. So good morning to you and your stale newspaper." And the lively, pretty little maiden bounded out of the room, carolling as she went, the words of the song,

"Liberty for me,
No man's wife I'll be," etc.

"Heartless girl!" were the words that burst from Henry's lips, as the door closed after her; and then, for a long time, he stood with his arms folded on his breast, and his head bowed, evidently in deep thought. "Yes, she is, indeed, heartless!" was the conclusion to which he came at last, and which seemed so certain, that, unconsciously, he uttered it aloud.

Never was he more in error. Julia Bradley was, by no means, a heartless girl. She was light-hearted, for nature had richly endowed her with a cheerful disposition, she was free from care, and untouched by sorrow. She differed from her cousin Henry in that she always saw first the bright side of any picture, while the dark side appeared first to him; she saw but the "silver lining"

of the cloud, while to him, whatever cloud
gloomed over his head was, indeed, but the
"blackness of darkness." Like the bee, she
drew honey from every flower, and knew
how to be happy under all circumstances.
But, although she laughed more than she
wept, and talked more in gay and jesting
language than in serious, measured phrase,
yet no one felt more keenly than she the mis-
eries of others, and few moved with such
alacrity to their relief. Innocent and guile-
less herself, she believed others to be so, and
lived in the blissfulness of childlike faith in
the world's goodness, and its constantly
increasing wisdom, while a knowledge of the
actual sin and oppression of the world gathered gloom upon the heart of her cousin,
and, at times, almost maddened his brain.
While his heart was like the "river sponge,
constantly saturated with the passing streams
of another's sorrow," hers was more like the
blessed sunlight, forever imparting warmth
and light to all who came under her influence. With true womanly intuition, she
fully comprehended the depths of her cousin's serious and somewhat stern nature ;
while he, with man's frequent obtuseness,
where woman is the object of scrutiny,

judged her to be heartless, weak, and superficial in character, if not feeble in intellect.

Henry was, however, more correct in his
estimate of the sewing society, concerning
which he expressed so much dissatisfaction.
Originally benevolent in its aim, and useful
in its results, it had sadly degenerated with
the influx of young and giddy people into its
midst. Amusement seemed now to be the
whole object for which the young people
met; for of these was the society mainly
composed, the elder and more sedate portion
of the body having withdrawn, in consequence of the introduction of somewhat
questionable amusements into the evening
entertainments. This secession had caused
much hard feeling, and many ill-natured remarks; while the young people, left more
free to follow their tastes than ever, by the
withdrawal of their elders, ran the giddiest
round of frolic and fun imaginable. It was
not long before the evening session of the
once staid, practical society, became characterized by an extravagance of display and
parade, a lawlessness of demeanor, and an
abandonment of the whole company to the
most riotous pleasure, that would have rendered obnoxious even a large and fashion-

able party in that somewhat quiet town. There was, indeed, need of reform. Julia had felt this for sometime, though she had said nothing of the sort, and was generally the gayest of the gay at these gatherings, the first at the society, and the last to leave it. Henry's strictures led her to carry out instantly a resolution she had been long forming — and in fifteen minutes after their conversation, above narrated, she had flung on hat and shawl, and started on her mission. It needed but few arguments from her, the village favorite, to convince the young people that a reformation was necessary in their sewing society, and but little persuasion to obtain from them a promise to aid in revolutionizing the little community that had so sadly deteriorated.

But it was a more difficult task to bring back the seceders from the society, and to restore the disaffected. They were older, firmer, and not so easily won. But who can long resist the influence of kind and gentle persuasion? Julia apologized to the senior ladies who had been shocked at the wild frolics of herself and young friends, promised amendment, portrayed graphically widow Foster's sufferings, and the aid that might be afforded her, would the matrons but return to their old posts, and coaxed and persuaded and removed obstacles — and gradually, the ice thawed from their manners and their hearts, and one after another consented " to be present at one more meeting of the society."

The next thing was to obtain widow Foster's permission for the society to meet with her, and aid her as they were able. This was easily effected. Now, although, really, Julia had accomplished all this herself, yet she had worked in such a way, that her agency, at the time, was hardly seen or acknowledged. She had conversed with one, reconciled another, won over a third, and then had led these to influence others in the same way, until, finally, the "whole lump was leavened;" and yet, it would have been difficult for even those influenced, to tell who was the prime mover in this reform.

Great was the stare of astonishment from those who were not in the secret, when, on the next sabbath, at the close of the afternoon service, the good minister read from the pulpit the secretary's notice, that " the next meeting of the ladies' sewing society would be held on the ensuing Wednesday, at the residence of Mrs. Foster." Henry cast a quick, sudden glance down the pew where his cousin sat, looking as demure as her mirth-loving eyes, and roguish mouth, round which the dimples were ever playing at "hide and seek" would permit—but her countenance revealed nothing. And when, afterwards, he inquired of her as to the originator of this new movement, he only learned from her that "some of the ladies had laid the plan;" notwithstanding which evasion, however, he saw through the whole, and his heart grew light in his bosom, as he recalled his decision of a few days before, and said to himself, "she is not heartless, after all."

Wednesday afternoon came—clear, bright and cool. An October sun shed down a most glorious and mellow light on the gorgeously apparelled forest, •on the brown fields, and rippling streams, whose music was so soon to be hushed, and whose dancing feet stayed by the fettering ice of winter. As early as one o'clock, the society began to assemble at the humble dwelling of widow Foster; for the etiquette that obtains so widely in cities, is little regarded in our country villages, and the earlier that companies assembling for an afternoon can get

together, the better. There was a general
turn-out of all who had ever been connected
with the society, and the little domicil of the
poor widow was crowded to its utmost
capacity. All came, bearing some substan-
tial present for the widow or her children, or
if any had failed to provide any other gift, a
broad piece of silver or a bank note was
thrust into the good woman's hand. Loads
of wood were thrown off into her wood-
house, a barrel of flour was rolled into her
kitchen, cotton cloth, flannel and calico were
laid upon her table, from which garments
were cut and fitted for the little ones, when
nimble fingers moved rapidly to complete
them, ready to wear. Eatables of all kinds
stored the shelves of the pantry, groceries
were packed away for future use, and at the
hour of supper, the festive board was heavily
laden with necessary food.

It was touching indeed, to witness Mrs.
Foster's gratitude. Poor woman! she had
toiled on for years, almost unaided and un-
friended, at times unable at the close of one
meal to tell where the next was to be obtained, yet in the depth of her darkness,
sorrow, and poverty, implicitly trusting in
the God of the widow and fatherless, who

had never failed her. But now, such a perfect avalanche of favors and blessings was heaped upon her that her heart was overwhelmed; and as one after another came, bearing some donation, grateful emotions choked her utterance, tears trickled down her thin cheeks, and she could only press the hands of the donors, and utter a fervent "God bless you!"

Little Ellen, the widow's second child, a girl of ten summers, whom consumption had led "to the boundaries of the spirit-land," sat bolstered up in a rocking-chair, the deadly hectic burning on her cheek, and the brilliance of consumption beaming from her eye. Now, a warm flannel wrapper was given the little girl; then some one sought to tempt her appetite with a transparent jelly, or a dainty confection; or a pretty book was placed in the emaciated little hand; or, which went to the heart of the little heaven-bound sufferer more than aught else, a soft hand stroked her smooth hair, warm lips pressed a kiss on her pale brow, and a voice of music spake to her the language of kindness and sympathy. Then the large dark eyes of the patient, dying child grew moist with feeling, and the faint, but eloquent smile that illuminated her wasted features, told of the angel spirit that animated the frail form.

It was astonishing how perfect was the happiness and unanimity that reigned among the members of that divided body, on that afternoon. All were pervaded with the same amiable spirit — both young and old, grave and gay — all chatted together, all worked together, and so busy and happy were they, that scandal was forgotten, and quarrels were laid aside. Even those, who, in their hearts, had sneered at the idea of a meeting at widow Foster's dwelling, that ill-looking, ill-furnished, unpainted, uncarpeted old tenement, were obliged to confess to themselves, that seldom had they passed, anywhere, a more agreeable afternoon.

In the evening, but not till eight o'clock, for the by-laws of the society were now to be strictly carried out, the gentlemen friends of the ladies made their appearance. Nothing was said of backgammon, whist, or dancing, yet it was found possible to pass an hour or so, agreeably, in pleasant conversation. Before they separated, Julia suggested the propriety of the gentlemen making a donation to the poor family, and instantly started round among them with Willie Fos-

ter's cap as a contribution box, into which a
little shower of silver coins was immediately
rained — for the gentlemen gallantly determined not to be outdone by the ladies.

While they were debating where to hold
the next meeting, the "heartless" Julia inti-
mated to the president of the society, that
she had ascertained by personal inquiry, that
old Mrs. Howard, who had outlived husband
and children, and who dwelt alone under the
hill, was entirely destitute of winter clothing,
and of means to obtain any; and immediately the worthy matron appointed the next
meeting at her own residence, begging all
the ladies to be in attendance, as they were
to work for old Mrs. Howard.

At the next meeting, the names of a number of young boys and girls were presented,
who were said to be deprived of the advantages of the district school, because they
lacked clothes to wear, and books to use —
and a vote was unanimously passed to supply
these deficiencies from the society's treasury,
which, now that the hearts of its members
were open, seemed like the purse of Fortu-
natus, in the fairy story, inexhaustible.

And thus, all through the winter, did the
society zealously labor. New life seemed to

animate it, and from having nothing to do, it passed to the opposite extreme, and became so crowded with work, that weekly meetings took the place of semi-monthly sessions, and even then, the ladies were straightened for time to accomplish all that their generous hearts devised. Many who had ever stood aloof from the institution came forward and joined it, helping with heart and hand; it rose in character, as it increased in numbers, and not unfrequent were the donations made to it by the town's people. Now there came a small sum of money, now a few yards of calico, or a piece of cotton cloth, while even the shopkeepers with whom the society traded, became so munificent as to sell to them at cost.

There was one place at which the society had long contemplated holding a meeting, but sickness in that household had prevented. This was at the residence of Mr. Lambert, who lived in a miserable dwelling just on the outskirts of the village. Mr. Lambert was unfortunately addicted to intemperance, and though capable of maintaining well his large family, and naturally kind-hearted and well-disposed, yet through his criminal self-indulgence, his poor wife and children were

were well-nigh reduced to beggary. Fruit-
less efforts had again and again been made
to effect his reformation, until he was, at
last, given up as lost by all who knew him,
and people only thought of aiding his family,
and of rendering them comfortable. This
was the sole object that the ladies' society
had in view, when it proposed to Mrs. Lambert to hold a meeting at her house — a prop-
osition to which the tired woman gratefully
acceded.

It was late in the spring before the dissipated father of this poor and sad family
recovered from an illness, brought on by his
excesses, which had confined him to his bed
all winter. But, at last, one warm, beautiful
May afternoon, when the balmy air was vo-
cal with the music of bird voices, the hum
of insects and the murmuring of rippling
streams, groups of the village matrons and
maidens might have been seen, on foot and
in carriages, laden with necessaries for the
needy family, now stepping cautiously over
the foot-worn bridge, and now climbing the
steep hill, on their way to the cheerless, com-
fortless home of the Lamberts. Much they
found to do that afternoon, for the mother's
energies were crippled by her great trials,

7

her spirit was crushed, and her heart well-
nigh broken, so that she had folded her
hands in inactivity, and sat down in indolent
despair, not even doing what, under more
favorable circumstances, she might have
done. But under the busy fingers of some
forty kind, willing, working women, garments grew as if by magic, and soon there
were completed frocks and pinafores for the
little girls, shirts and roundabouts for the
boys, articles of bed-clothing, and such apparel as the father and mother most needed.
Forth from a basket, of dimensions little less
than infinite, one good dame produced a
donation of stockings of various sizes; another, from a pocket nearly as capacious
drew a vest for the ruined father; while a
third untied a huge bundle handkerchief, and
discovered a neat cap and bonnet for the
mother. And then the provisions for the
inner man! "the edibles and potables!" there
surely could have been found no greater
quantity, even at the crowded village inn.
A faint gleam of sunshine came once more
to the pale, wan cheek of the drunkard's
wife, and light and laughter beamed dimly
again from the eyes of his haggard babes.
Yet there was a settled look of dejection on

the care-worn face of the wife, that told of
the agony tugging at her heart strings, of
the bitterness of the cup whose dregs she
had not yet drained. And on the beautiful
foreheads of the innocent children sat ever a
timid yet appealing expression, that might
have found utterance in the language,

"Our father's a drunkard, '*but we're not to blame!*'"

That father! never writhed mortal man in
more agony than he that afternoon. Like
the fabled Prometheus he was chained securely to one spot, while the ever-devouring
vulture of remorse preyed pitilessly on his
heart. Few went within the little bedroom
where he lay upon his couch, and those few
seemed by their laconic address and freezing
manner to express rebuke and dislike. He
saw the happy matrons and maidens as they
passed his narrow door, and memory brought
up from the abyss of the past, the form and
face of his now sorrowful wife, when they
were as fresh and blooming as the gladdest
and brightest of her guests—the time when
fortune smiled upon him, and men gave him
their hands in confidence, when his home
was happy and his heart light—and the con-
trast between that bright past and the

gloomy present was so painful, that perspi-
ration was forced out upon his brow, and
low moans of agony wrung from his heart.
What he had been, what he was, and what
he ought to be, all came up before him, and
so intense was his anguish that he envied the
very dead who slept calmly in the graveyard.

Tea was announced, and as the company
were passing to the kitchen, where the tables
were spread, Julia Bradley turned her head
towards the room of the sick man, when she
saw, or thought she saw him dash away a
tear. Pity for him was her first emotion,
and then a good thought came into her
mind, and she lingered behind the rest to
carry it into action. Softly, and with a
pleasant smile, she stepped to the bed of the
invalid, and with her silvery voice accosted
him. Language of sympathy and commiseration he was not used to, and it went to
his heart. Expressions of interest in himself he had not heard for a long time, and
all form of reply was choked down by his
emotions. But when the good-hearted girl
spoke lovingly of his wife and children, and
praised the beauty and intelligence of the
latter, and the industry and activity of the
former, the husband and father were moved

within him, and he wept. Julia had touched
the right chord in his bosom.

"No man ever had a better wife or finer
children, and, God knows, I wish they were
rid of me entirely, as they will be, before
long—for then they'll be better off;" was
his earnest remark.

"I've been thinking of a plan to benefit
your family very much, only I fear you will
not fall in with it," said Julia, hardly daring
to broach the subject nearest her heart at
this moment.

"Don't you think I love my wife and children?" was the blunt rejoinder.

"Oh, yes, I know you do, as well as any
man—as you love your own life; but my plan
involves some sacrifice."

"And do you think I would not make it?
I would make any sacrifice for my family—
I would lay down my life for them!"

"Oh, dear sir," replied Julia with solemn
earnestness, "if you would but make *this*
sacrifice, if you would but lay away, at once
and forever, not your life, but your death—
that which destroys yourself, makes miserable your good wife and innocent babes who
yet dearly love you, and who cling to you
when others cast you off! Oh, sir, give up

but this one habit, and how happy a household will yours become!"

A torrent of tears rained down the poor man's face at this earnest appeal, and he trembled violently, but said not a word.

"Why not abjure forever that poison which has already wrought such woe in your house? Think how easily you can become the man you once were, how easily you can again make your wife and children happy! You have but to resolve to become a temperate, sober man, and to keep that resolution, and the good work is done! Why not make such a resolution? Oh, sir, do, for your wife's and children's sake!"

A sudden change passed over poor Lambert's face; a look of firmness supplanted the listless, sad expression that was on his countenance but a moment before, his lips became compressed tightly, and he struck with his closed hand energetically upon the bed, saying, "I *will* resolve! I *do*, I *will* promise!"

"Let me write it," said Julia, eagerly; and catching up a New Testament that lay on the table at the side of the bed, with her pencil, she wrote on the blank leaf as follows:

"I do most solemnly promise, in the presence of Almighty God, that I will never again drink anything that will intoxicate."

Mr. Lambert took the volume from her hand, read slowly what she had written, and then taking her proffered pencil, wrote underneath, in a bold hand, with a firmness that indented several pages, "JAMES LAMBERT." "So help me God, I will never break that promise, Miss Bradley," said he, handing back the book.

"Oh, thank you, sir! Bless you, sir! Bless you! I am *sure* you will never break it!" and the overjoyed girl pressed the brawny hand of the inebriate between both hers, hardly conscious in her ecstasy of what she was about. Smiles broke over her face, and she turned away to hide the tears of which she had no cause to be ashamed. Hope and resolution lighted up the eyes of the sick man, and excitement brought a warm color to his cheek, so that he seemed almost well again.

But a third party had witnessed this little scene, and in *her* heart was deeper, more grateful joy than in Julia's. Mrs. Lambert had missed the good girl from the tea-table, and having come in quest of her, had beheld all that had transpired. A slight movement at the door called thither the attention of the husband and of Julia, and there stood the completely overwhelmed wife, big tears dropping like summer rain from her face, with upraised hands clasped tightly from intense feeling, her lips parted, and the paleness of excitement blanching yet whiter her ever pale features. "Oh, my dear James! my dear, *dear* husband!" burst from her overcharged heart, as she rushed towards the bed; and winding her arms about his neck, she sobbed on his pillow like a very infant. The sufferings of past years, his deep debasement, his harsh treatment of herself and little ones, his neglect of his family—all, all were forgotten, the tenderness of their early affection came back in all its freshness, and the lips of the so long unhappy, and almost alienated couple, met in a kiss.

It was soon known by all in the house that Mr. Lambert had pledged himself never again to drink, and, greatly to Julia's annoyance, the circumstances connected with it flew like wildfire from lip to lip. All was excitement. Some hurried to Mr. Lambert's room to offer their congratulations, and to strengthen his newly formed resolution; others gathered around Julia, stunning her with praises and thanks, while the children of the family stood at a distance, and looked up at the fair girl, as though she were a goddess, whom they must worship afar off.

That evening, when the gentlemen came to gallant home their wives, sisters, cousins, and *friends*,—a duty they never failed to perform,—Henry Marston, for the first time, made his appearance at the sewing society. The occurrence of the afternoon furnished the topic of conversation for the evening; and Julia, poor girl, was again greatly distressed at the laudation of which she was the object, and at the exaggerated praise of herself that came from all lips. All her previous good deeds were dragged to light, and she became the lion of the evening, "the observed of all observers." Cousin Henry sought her out, and commended her as he had never done before, mildly, but warmly, and her eyes were bent to the ground by the undisguised admiration and affection that beamed from his.

"I believe you promised to join us, cousin Henry," she said, on their way home that night, "when our society became more useful. Are we not sufficiently utilitarian to suit your notions now?"

"Dear Julia! what a good girl you are! How this sewing society has changed, and all through your instrumentality! How have I wronged you, by calling you vain and heartless! Forgive me, dearest cousin, for until recently, I have never understood you."

"But all this is not to the purpose, Henry. Don't wander from the question. I am secretary of the society; say, will you give me your name?"

"Yes, Julia," he replied, with a vehemence that almost startled her; "and not my name merely, but my hand and my heart. Will you accept them? Do not say no, for my happiness depends upon your answering yes. Tell me that my years of unspoken affection are not unrequited, and promise, gladsome, light-hearted cousin, as my own dear wife, to infuse into my darker and less hopeful nature, the sunshine and happiness that dwell in your heart. Oh Julia, be mine, and teach me, like yourself, to make the world better for my having lived in it!"

After what the fair reader has learned of Julia's benevolent nature, it will easily be believed that she complied with so reasonable a request. But we are not skillful in depicting love scenes, and must leave Julia's reply entirely to the imagination of the gentle reader. Just go back a few years, and recall your own language and manner under similar circumstances, or forward a few years, and think how you *will* act, and what you *will* say, when her case becomes your own, and you will have Julia's answer, at least, in substance. But this we will tell you: there was a wedding at the village church that fall, at which were present all the members of the sewing society, Widow Foster, and her little ones, as well as the Lamberts, who would, on no account, have been absent from the bridal of their benefactress.

LA PUEBLA DE LOS ANGELOS.

["We explored the cathedral, of which mortals had built the
walls, and which angels had capped with a mighty dome, of a
symmetry and perfection in stonework unequalled by human
builders. In gratitude to the supernatural architects, the city
has since been called 'LA PUEBLA DE LOS ANGELOS,' or 'AN-
GEL CITY.'"]

Deep they laid the strong foundations,
　High the massive walls upreared,
And the tall and sculptured columns
　Marble forest-trees appeared.
Out from these the groined arches
　Sprang in grace and strength o'erhead;
And a high and vaulted ceiling
　Gave the heart a sense of dread,
　Stretching dim above the head.

Then they built the lofty altar,
　Whence the incense-flame might rise;
Here the holy cross was planted,
　For the sinner's tearful eyes.
And they hollowed shadowed niches,
　To enshrine the statues rare,
Which, with pale hands ever folded,
　Seem outpouring ceaseless prayer,
　Of the hallowed place aware.

Then they sank the tinted window
　　Far within the massive wall,
That, subdued, the slanting sunbeams
　　Through the pillared aisles might fall.
And they crowned each arching buttress
　　With a tall and gilded spire,
To reflect the ruddy morning,
　　Or the glorious sunset fire,
　　　When glows red day's funeral pyre.

Never lagged the weary workmen,
　　Who, with pious zeal elate,
Raised to God a holy temple,
　　To his worship consecrate.
Never lacked they gold or silver,
　　Never lacked they jewels rare;
And a soft and shining splendor
　　Was infused into the air,
　　　From the gold and jewels rare.

So they wrought, till all was ended,
　　Save the dome that capped the whole,
When the builders, worn and weary,
　　Rested from their lengthened toil.
Night dropped down her starry curtain,
　　Midnight hushed the world to rest,
When, adown the rifted heavens,
　　Softer than the rosiest west,
　　　Came the angels of the blest.

Brighter than the woven moonlight
　　Were the robes the angels wore;
Brighter than the sun of noonday
　　Were the implements they bore.

All that night, a murmured music
Rippled out upon the air;
All that night, the heavenly builders
Toiled with superhuman care,
Toiled with skill and beauty rare.

Mortal hands could ne'er have framed it,
That unique and gorgeous dome;
Angels only could have planned it,
In their wondrous angel-home.
Toiled they on till dawn of morning,
Noiseless, save their heavenly lay,
When, complete, the dome was burnished
With the sunlight's earliest ray,
And the angels fled the day.

Came once more the pious builders,
With their zeal and strength new-born;
But, behold! the dome, completed,
Had already kissed the morn!
Bright and dazzling was the radiance
From the gilded roof that streamed;
And the cross made dim the sunlight
With the brilliance of its beam! —
Was it thus, or did they dream?

On their knees they sank in wonder,
On their knees they sank in prayer;
"Sure," they said, "God's holy angels
In the night have labored here.
Let us call it ANGEL CITY,
Where the Holy Ones have wrought;
And let rare and votive offerings
To the sacred place be brought.—
Do the angels know our thought?"

Ay, 't is so. Encamping round us,
　Angels list whate'er we say;
And they come and go about us,
　In the night-time and the day.
Doubt not, if thy aim be holy,
　They will aid thee in thy need;
Doubt not they are watching o'er thee, .
　When true purpose shapes thy deed.—
　Trust the angels when they lead.

LOST AND FOUND.

The softness and stillness of a summer night rested like a blessing upon the little village of N——, that, nested in foliage, redolent of flower sweets, and glittering with dew, was now hushed in deep slumber. The hour of midnight was passed; the declining moon hung on the edge of the western horizon, magnified, golden and glorious, while a thousand calm stars shone serenely from the blue above. Not a light beamed from the windows of the village, save where a few feeble rays struggled dimly through the curtained casement of the sick room, and not a sound broke the holy quiet which had lapped the world in Elysian slumber, except the tinkling of the rivulets and the gurgling of the brooks along their pebbly channels, the occasional note of a bird from its nest in the branches, and the distant plaint of the whippoorwill.

It was at this still hour that Charles Vin-

ton entered his native town and wended his
way to the residence of his father. Now in
the moonlight, now in the shadow, here,
across sweet-scented, dewy fields, there,
along the worn and dusty highway, over
fences, bridges and walls, through orchards,
barn-yards and gardens, evidently coveting
secrecy, and seeking to abridge the distance
lying between himself and his destination as
much as possible, he kept on his way till he
stood in front of the paternal mansion. As
he proceeded up the tree-lined, graveled avenue to the dwelling, Growler, the house-dog,
sprang from his kennel with a furious chal-
lenge; but, as he approached the intruder,
his fierce bark of assault was softened into a
growl of recognition and a loving whine;
and leaping upon the young man, he nearly
overwhelmed him with demonstrations of
good will. Returning the dog's caresses, the
youth walked sadly and pensively around the
house and its grounds, his canine friend
bearing him company. He passed into the
garden, a miracle of taste and beauty, and
walked among the beds of flowers that his
sister's own fair hands tended, plucking here
a pansy, and there a forget-me-not, which
were deposited within the leaves of his mem-

orandum book; he sought the stable, and the stall of the old family horse, and laid his head caressingly upon the neck of the petted animal, as was his wont when a boy, till memory of his childhood's days brought a tear to his eye that trickled down upon the mane of old Roan: then he stole round to the front of the house, where he could command the windows of the apartment occupied by his parents. Here he gazed long and wishfully,—for his hopes had unconsciously taken counsel of his desires, and he almost expected the white curtain would be lifted, and that he should see his mother's face gazing down fondly into his own once more. But he turned away at last, murmuring feelingly, and with tears: "Mother, dear mother! *can* I go without seeing you?" Then, round to the side of the mansion he crept, to the low windows of his sister's bedroom, and pulling aside the sweetbrier that clambered over the blinds, he thrust a note through its closed slats, and sorrowfully, like Adam quitting Paradise, turned his steps away from his home, out into the world again. Down the graveled, shady walk, out into the highway and along the dusty road, he held his way, Growler yet walking beside him, not turning even to glance at the cottage home of her who had been his playmate in boyhood, and who had since become dearer to him than all the world beside. No, he quickened his steps as though the tender associations connected with the neighborhood were transformed into avenging furies, whose scorpion whips were scourging him onward; and without even a farewell look to the home of his gentle Lucy, he hurried up the hill, to its summit.

Here he stayed his flight, and turning, looked back. Outstretched before him lay the village where he was born, where he had played in childhood, where dwelt those dearer to him than life. The tall-spired church, where he had sat beside his parents and sister, Sabbath after Sabbath—the school house, with its play ground and its little belfry—the streams, where he had fished—the orchards, where he had spent many a long summer day in plays and happy indolence—the meadows, where he had tumbled among the heaps of new-made hay—his own home, with its barns, stables, garden, trees and shrubbery—the home of Lucy Carlton—*her* home, whose name he hardly dared breathe

8H

now in his disgrace, even to himself—all these were before him, and he gazed long and earnestly. It might have been five minutes that he stood there, and it might have been an hour—Charles Vinton could not have told, for he took no cognizance of time. Memory, conscience and affection were busy within, and he was listening to their still voices. There was something in the place, the hour, and the associations of the moment that went to his soul; aspirations after better things than had been the pursuit of his youth thus far, filled his heart; and as he stood there in the gray of the coming dawn, underneath the open canopy of heaven, with no eye upon him but God's, and no witnesses but the starry sentinels above, his soul uttered a wordless renunciation of the folly, madness and dissipation of his past life, that had exiled him from home and happiness, and brought sorrow to the hearts of those who loved him, and he vowed henceforth to be a MAN—a man in its noblest, truest, highest sense. That renunciation—that vow, were registered in heaven.

Stooping to the faithful dog, that, weary of waiting for his young master to proceed, had crouched beside him, he wound his arms

about his neck, pressed his shaggy head to
his cheek, and weeping, addressed him in
tones of endearment, such as a mother loves
to use to her babe, "And now go, Growler!
good dog, go! good by! you can't go with
me, so go back! go back!" and he urged the
unwilling brute, till he turned slowly towards
his home. Then—one more look of farewell
—one more speechless, earnest adjuration to
his spirit to keep the vow it had made—one
passionate invocation of blessing upon his
angelic mother, and upon her whose name
he shrank from uttering—and Charles Vinton commenced the descent of the hill on the
other side, and soon lost sight of the town
of his nativity—perhaps forever. On he
walked rapidly, for miles, till he gained a
railroad station; and here he halted till the
coming of the puffing, whizzing, smoking
locomotive, with its train of cars, on its early
way to New-York, the commercial emporium
of our country, when he took passage for the
great metropolis.

It would be difficult to say which heart
was heavier the next morning—Charles Vinton's, or his sister Emily's. The note thrust
through the blind was immediately perceived
by her, on withdrawing the curtain, and to

her astonishment and distress she read the following half sad, half comic letter:

"DEAR SISTER EMILY:—I have 'taken Time by the forelock,' and though only in my Sophomore year, have graduated from college on my own hook. To be sure, I cannot boast of 'the honors' that I have borne away, as I have only the honor of expulsion; nor have the faculty awarded me a '*sheepskin*,' nor the title of A. B.; but *n'importe;* I can get along without them.

A party of us rendered the trustees some unsolicited service in their building operations. They were about to tear down some out-buildings, and erect better; and to facilitate matters we put a few pounds of powder under the half-tumbled-down houses, and sent them to Jericho, sky-rocket fashion. Some little damage was done, and as a warning to all lovers of fun and gunpowder explosions, five of us received our walking tickets—myself among the number. *Eh bien! puisque j'ai fait la faute, c'est a moi d'en porter la peine.* Except for the sake of my friends, I do not regret my expulsion, for from the days when I blubbered over *hic, hæc, hoc,* of my Latin grammar, and the verb *tupto* of my Greek, and halted at the *pons asinorum* of Euclid, till fairly whipped over it by my teacher, have I rebelled at the idea of going to college. This you very well know. As to a profession, the deuce take the whole of them for all me. I have neither 'clean hands, nor pure heart' enough for the ministry; I detest all those 'gentlemen of the green bag,' those dry fellows, Coke, Blackstone, Hale, Lyttleton, and the whole posse of them; and as to passing my days in pestilential sick-rooms, and druggist shops, in counting pulses, compounding medicines, administering potions, preparing pills, and spreading plasters—ugh! I'd never be a physician.

I know my father too well to believe he would deviate from the course he threatened to pursue; and being certain that he would 'turn me out of doors' if I should venture under his roof, I have resolved to get the start of him, and to exile myself. I shall see his face no more.

Dear sister, our father is a good man, but towards me he has been both unjust and severe. He would make me what God and nature never intended me for — a lawyer, a book-worm, a walking encyclopedia. I would be a busy worker in the world — a mechanic, or a trader. Father would lay me on the Procrustean bed of his wishes, and stretch me out, or cut me off, according as my proportions are longer or shorter than those of his ideal. It is against this that I protest.

But, sister, though I am now an outcast, an alien by my father's decision, which *will not* be revoked, I will yet be *something* in the world. From this very first day of my hegira, I will turn over a new leaf; I have done sowing 'wild oats;' I shall now begin to be a man. You may *never* hear of me again; but if you do, you shall hear what will not make you blush for me.

Ah me! what shall I say to my mother, my blessed mother, who loves me so tenderly, who will grieve so at my disgrace, who has ever been to me like an angel! Oh, if my father had been like her, I might have been a better man! At this very moment, Emily, my heart is yearning towards her. I never loved her more! The tears are wetting my cheek while I write, and I long to throw myself into my mother's arms, as when a child! Sister, crave forgiveness of her for me; and for your sakes, blessed mother, dear sister, I will in the future atone for the past — I will retrieve the character that I have lost. Hear me, oh heaven, for I promise it before thee!

There is one other, Emily, whom my disgrace will affect; her love I have forfeited — she will despise me. Give her the enclosed note.

And now, good by, mother and sister. Remember me, and though undeserving, continue to love me. I have my mother's miniature — it will go with me' everywhere, my *vade mecum.* It will be a talisman against all evil, it will be my Mentor when enticed to wrong. Good by."   "CHARLES."

The other note was to Lucy Carlton, and was more brief. It ran thus:

"DEAR LUCY: — You may have learned before this that I am expelled from college, for a character-istic act of fool-hardiness. I have sorely tried your affection heretofore, and I know now that this dis-grace will rear a wall of partition between us. Be it so. I know too well my own unworthiness and your goodness to dare ask for aught else. This note is merely to say 'Good by' to you, for I shall not return to my father's house at present — perhaps *never* shall.

And now good by, Lucy; you are free from the early betrothal that has made me happy for a few short years. Although my own foolishness has ren-dered it null and void, I am distressed that it is can-celled. There is exquisite anguish in the thought that I have lost you by my folly — that you will de-spise, renounce and forget me — *you*, whom I have loved from boyhood — *you*, whom I love at this mo ment with all the untamed energy of a passionate nature — *you*, Lucy, for whom I could lay down life itself! I deserve only your contempt and aversion. I can reasonably expect nothing more. Farewell!"   "CHARLES VINTON."

With tears and silent agony Emily Vinton perused again and again her brother's letter, and still she sat in her little bedroom and wept over it, ignorant how to communicate the sad intelligence to her parents. But as she still sobbed with her face buried in the pillow, she caught the sound of her father's voice in loud and angry tones in an adjoining room; and as the thought flashed across her mind that Charles might have acquainted him with his expulsion, by means of a note, she hastened her toilet, and joined her father, to speak in her brother's behalf if necessary, as she had often done before.

Mr. Vinton was pacing the room in an excited manner when Emily entered, while her mother, pale and anxious, was poring over a letter, a glance at which sufficed to convince her that the penmanship was other than her brother's. It was an official letter informing Mr. Vinton of his son's expulsion from college. Nothing could exceed the father's indignation; it was frightful to witness; neither his wife or daughter could check the torrent of his wrath, and when Emily produced her epistle from the erring one, the father ran through the first paragraph, and then dashing the note to the ground, refused to read or hear more, and commanded Emily, to cease her excuses and pleas for him.

"Hear him?" cried the infuriated man; "hear him! he makes light of his disgrace, he turns his expulsion into ridicule! By heavens! but that fellow is enough to stir

older blood than mine! Let me hear no
more of him! I disown him! I disinherit
him! He is to me as if he were dead!
From this day I have no child but Emily!
Do not mention his name in my presence
again, and let the worthless vagabond be
caught again on my premises—that's all!"
Sorry words these for a father to utter concerning a child.

Not thus was Mrs. Vinton affected; she
was overwhelmed with grief. For a time
her agony was so intense, it seemed as if it
would kill her. She had always feared lest
her wild, impulsive, passionate boy, whose
tastes and wishes were wholly at variance
with his father's, would fall under that father's ban; and tremblingly had she watched
the gathering of that storm which had now
burst upon them in such fury, unable to avert
it. But now, how her heart went out after
her erring boy! It was agony to her to
think that he was cast out friendless, penniless and alone, to the tender mercies of a
cold world; and her heart died within her
as she thought of the want and privation to
which he must necessarily be subjected, if
standing alone in the world. Oh, how she
longed to fold him to her heart! How her

THE LOST AND FOUND. 115

arms reached out involuntarily, as if to en-
circle him! With what touching, endearing
epithets she coupled his name! *Could* she
be reconciled to the thought that she might
never again see her beautiful Charles, who
was so generous in his impulses, so joyous in
spirit, so full of frolic and fun? who possessed such boundless energy of character, and
such a large, warm heart? Was there no
clue to his location? Could not her voice
of persuasion and affection reach him? It
must be that he would return, and his father
must be softened to forgiveness! Never,
never could she abandon him—never could
her heart close against him. And the anguish of the poor, restless, almost heart-
broken mother was pitiable.

There was yet another to whom this de-
fection of Charles Vinton came with a
blighting power. This one was Lucy Carlton. Too sad herself to communicate in
language the great grief that weighed heavily on both, Emily Vinton placed both letters
in her hand, and bade her read. Rapidly
her eye ran over both notes, while the color
of her cheek faded and faded, till she was
whiter than marble. Yet on she read, to the
very last word, and though a tear trembled

on her eyelid, she did not weep, and though her cheek was blanched to a startling whiteness, she did not faint. "Oh Charles, how little you have understood me!" was the only utterance she gave to her feelings in the presence of Emily; but from that day Lucy Carlton was changed. There was no ado, no violent outburst of feeling, no passionate words, no hysterical weeping—but the paleness that came to her cheek at the announcement of Charles' departure, became habitual to her, till all ceased to ascribe it to ill health. In a few weeks she moved about in the discharge of her duties as calmly as ever, sought less the solitude of her room, and retired less to lonely haunts in the forest— but her girlish joyousness was fled forever. The whole ebb and flow of her feelings were revulsed, and in her world of emotion and affection a mighty chasm had been rent, that ever after was unfilled. *That* day became an epoch in her life—for on that day she waked suddenly from a dream of bliss to dream no more; that day brought an abrupt transition from happy maidenhood, with its dreamy fancies, its budding hopes, and rosy atmosphere, to suffering, enduring, patient womanhood. A new tie seemed to spring

up between her and the mother and sister of
him whom she loved—a tie born of a common sorrow; and Lucy Carlton became almost one of the family.

Mr. Vinton, though naturally a fond father,
was yet stern and inflexible, impetuous and
excitable. For months, and perhaps years,
his anger burned fiercely against his son,
who fully inherited his father's fiery nature;
and even when milder feelings came to his
heart, and he half repented his severity towards his child, his lips were hermetically
sealed concerning him, and none knew of
the father's relenting.

He had erred greatly in the education of
his child. From his infancy he had destined
him for a profession; and though, as the
boy's character developed, he perceived his
disinclination to the life of a student, in no
wise did it change his purpose. He dealt
with him as if he were a mere machine,
which it was only necessary to wind up, in
order for it to work in this or that direction;
and while the boy looked longingly to the
workshops and stores at whose benches and
counters he saw other youths of his age, he
was despatched to school, and forced into
studies that were detestable to him. Ever

first and foremost in all boyish sports and athletic exercises, Charles Vinton was the last in his class; and during his irksome confinement in the school room, his roguish, fun-loving nature was constantly active, greatly to the annoyance of his teachers and the delight of his companions.

After incredible pains on the part of his tutors, and incredible drudgery and heart-burning on his own, he was declared fitted for college. Active, muscular, full of life, longing for emancipation from the school room, its tasks and governors, catching the sound of conflict, strife and endeavor that came to him like sweetest music from the bustling world, as the "war-horse smelleth the battle afar off," Charles protested earnestly against his father's determination, and begged for a chance in the mercantile or mechanical world, in either of which departments he would have excelled. Mr. Vinton was inexorable; one might as well have tried to turn back the incoming tide as to have changed his darling purpose; and, cursing Homer, Horace, Virgil and Ovid, Xenophon, Plato, Livy and Sallust, Euclid, Legendre, Newton and La Place, and vowing eternal hatred to themes and theses, epics and pastorals, problems and propositions, the reluctant youth was despatched to a distant university.

It was only through the softening influences of home that the frolicsome, impulsive nature of the young man was held in check; consequently, when removed from the restraining influences of his mother and sister, when deprived of the sanctifying environments of home, his lawless, tameless, unbridled propensities were left free to run their wildest race. Heart and hand he joined every mad-cap adventure that was planned, was the first to start in a frolic, and the last to leave it, soon lost caste with the faculty, and obtained the unenviable reputation of being the veriest "scape-grace" in the institution. Twice was he suspended during his Freshman year; and his father, who saw in all this only determined opposition to his will and authority, had twice received him with dire displeasure and fearful anathemas, threatening him with disinheritance if the offence was repeated. But certain as was Charles Vinton that his father's threat would be executed, he yet kept on his giddy course, and before the close of his Sophomore year, was expelled. The consequence of this expulsion we have already seen.

Time rolled away after the flight of the disgraced student, and the lapse of years brought a sanative to the hearts of those most deeply wounded by his folly and its consequences. The place of Emily Vinton in her father's house was rendered vacant, for her bright face carried its sunshine to the home, and her fair form its grace to the hearthstone of another, whom she called "husband." Thus deprived of both her children, loneliness would have been Mrs. Vinton's portion, but for the daughter-like attentions and affection of Lucy Carlton, who clung to the sorrowing woman as though it were the last hold of her affections. Many sought the pale, shrinking girl, for there was in her face and manner a nameless charm, a certain *je ne sais quoi* which gained the love of all; and it was deemed passing strange that all suitors were alike unsuccessful. A calm, but kind refusal was steadily given to all who asked her hand or heart — and the world looked on and wondered that she preferred her lonely maiden life to the joys of happy wifehood. Alas! the world knew not that her heart was wandering, wandering ever over billows and waves, mountains and seas, to the dear, hapless alien in whose hand she had laid her own, with the promise to "love through all things." It knew not that her prayers went up nightly for him, and that no guilt, no disgrace, no sorrow, could ever divorce her from her allegiance to him.

There was one who shared her secret—that one was Mrs. Vinton. Together they sat in the purple twilight, and in the darkening evening, talking of days that were gone, bringing from the treasure-house of memory many a grateful reminiscence of the wanderer—many an affecting incident of his life—many a kind word and good deed that had cheered their hearts, till tears choked their utterance, and they wept on one another's necks. And then each tried to soothe the other with endearments that caused the tears to flow faster, and the heart to ache with a more remorseless pain; and each whispered hopes concerning the return of the prodigal, that to both seemed deceitful.

Oh, weary years! how slowly they rolled away, marking their progress by the snows they scattered on the head of the poor mother, by the furrows they ploughed upon her brow, and by the roses they stole from the cheek of Lucy Carlton. They numbered fif-

9

teen at last — and all hope of Charles Vinton's return was abandoned by his friends.
If living, they feared what was yet worse,
that he was morally dead; and though a
painful void was in their hearts, and an
agonizing memory poisoned every pleasant
draught of their lives, they bowed to the
Chastener and murmured not. To Mrs. Vinton, these long years of trial and suspense
had brought terrible suffering, and health
and physical vigor were ruined by it. It
seemed as though she would soon be called
to exchange the trials of life for the joys of
heaven; and believing that death was not
far in the distance, a desire seemed to spring
up in the heart to gather under her own roof,
once more before her departure, all her near
friends and kindred. It was perhaps a singular wish, but none opposed it, and preparations were made for a large family party at
the approaching Christmas.

The doors of the mansion had formerly
been opened ·on frequent festal occasions;
but during the fifteen previous years, fes-
tivity and hilarity had been strangers in Mr.
Vinton's house. But now Mrs. Vinton made
a temporary truce with sickness, sorrow, and
sad memories, and rallied herself to minister

to the happiness of others. Lucy Carlton was pressed into the service, and under the auspices of the tasteful, thoughtful girl, the preparations for Christmas went on right merrily. Holly, evergreen, running pine and spruce were brought from the woods to dec orate the parlors in true Christmas style; immense quantities of cakes and candies were prepared, of sweetmeats and fruits, of puddings and pastry. Last, but not least, a huge *bona fide* pine tree was transplanted from the forest to the front parlor, on the top of which Lucy placed the figure of an angel, which the children verily believed was the *Christ-Kindlein* himself; while the boughs were ladened with heterogeneous fruit — toys, books, bonbons and *confitures* — all for the grandchildren of Mr. and Mrs. Vinton, and their innumerable grand-nephews and nieces.

The evening preceding the long-anticipated festival had arrived, and though it was near midnight, Mrs. Vinton and Lucy were still in the parlors, putting the finishing touch to their preparations. But finally the last taper was affixed to the boughs of the Christmas tree, its last labelled gift was appended to the branches, and Lucy removed

to a little distance to contemplate the result
of their labors, while Mrs. Vinton, wearied,
sank into a chair, and burying her face in
her hands gave way to the sad thoughts and
feelings that rushed over her like a flood.
Tears sprang also to the eyes of Lucy, for
she divined that the thoughts of the mother
were with her son.   Both were started from
their revery, however, by a gentle knock at
the outer door, that would not have been
heard but for the deep stillness.   Mrs. Vinton's hands dropped from her face, and both
she and Lucy remained in a listening attitude
for a moment or two, when the rap was repeated.

"Who can it be?" said Mrs. Vinton; "it
is an unusual hour for a rap at the front
door: I will go;" and swinging wide the parlor door, for the hall lamp was extinguished,
she turned the key in the lock, and looked
out into the avenue.   As she peered cautiously out into the darkness, the tall figure
of a man advanced a step or two, a hand
was extended, and a voice tremulous with
feeling uttered the one, dear word, "Mother!"   But it was enough; that word was the
open sesame to the heart of Mrs. Vinton.
"Charles! Charles!" she feebly articulated,

and winding her arms about his neck, fell
faintly on his breast. Taking her in his
arms, the powerful man bore her to the parlor, and placing her on the sofa, bent over
her tenderly. "Oh, my dear boy!" she continued to say, holding him by the hand, as
if fearful that she might again lose him; "my
dear child! my poor wandering boy! God
be thanked that you are alive! Father in
heaven, 't is enough! 't is enough! Now I
am willing to die! Lucy, dear Lucy! God
has been better to us than our fears!
Charles, you have not forgotten Lucy Carlton?" Charles turned eagerly around, for
his mother's presence had banished every
other thought from his mind, and his emotion had blinded him, that he did not perceive the motionless, pallid girl. He advanced to offer his hand, but poor Lucy, who
had borne up under trouble and sorrow,
under years of trial and suffering, was con-
quered by her sudden joyful surprise; her
eyes became dim, her strength departed, and
she sank like yielding wax to the floor. Her
swoon was long and protracted; both Mrs.
Vinton and Charles were in agony.

"Oh! Charles," said Mrs. Vinton, "she
has mourned deeply over your absence; nev-

er was there so faithful a heart! God grant
that joy may not kill her!"

With tears, with passionate kisses, with
tenderest endeavors, Charles Vinton used
every means to restore the insensible Lucy;
and his efforts were at last rewarded by seeing her blue eyes unsealed, and by hearing
her offer thanksgiving to heaven for his return. Blessed hour! after fifteen years of
struggling with life, of buffeting its waves,
and tossing on its billows, the wanderer was
in the haven of his early home, with those
dearest to him beside him.

Till the dawn of the late morning there
they sat—the happy trio—while Charles re-
counted to his dear audience his many adventures. How they wept and smiled as he
told them of his many weeks' unsuccessful
endeavors to obtain employment in New
York! How they rejoiced when he told
them that he finally obtained a clerkship in
a Southern city, from which place, after having served as clerk for four or five years, he
went out as agent in one of the vessels own-
ed by his employers, to South America;
where, finding it possible to amass a fortune
in a few years, he had pitched his tent till
the present time, having been successful,

pecuniarily, beyond his most avaricious desires! And how proudly his mother looked upon him, as he solemnly averred that from the day he left home he had been guilty of no act of which he was now ashamed, or which his father, severe critic as he was, would censure! And how they anathematized all mail arrangements, and post-office departments, when he informed them that he had written again and again during the last fifteen years, and receiving no answer, had concluded that he was forgotten and unforgiven, and that under the influence of this belief he had hung round the house for hours that evening, not daring to enter, till from the windows he saw his mother weeping, and *felt* that it must be for him! And how his mother kissed his cheek and brow and lips, and Lucy wept on his shoulder, as he asked if he was indeed forgiven and loved fondly as-ever! Blessed moments! how they atoned for years of suffering! how years of enjoyment were compressed into their narrow limits! All felt that their happiness could only be exceeded by the bliss of that moment when the pilgrim of earth is ushered into the noontide glory of heaven!

It was deemed advisable for Mrs. Vinton

to prepare her husband's mind to receive his son, for though it was evident that as years had lulled his passions, and cooled the fever of his blood, he had relented towards his child, and regretted his severity, yet none knew his present feelings, or if the past would be cancelled under the circumstances. The family sat down as usual to the breakfast table, except that Mrs. Vinton and Lucy seemed by their radiant faces to have been quaffing the very Elixir of Life. Notwithstanding the sleepless night they had passed, their eyes beamed, their cheeks glowed, and their spirits overflowed.

"We'll have a Christmas party every month," said Mr. Vinton, setting down his coffee to gaze at the wonderful transformation of his wife and Lucy! "it's the best cosmetic yet. Why, wife, Lucy and you look ten years younger than you did yesterday! We'll have parties often after this, hey?"

"We are both very happy in prospect of our party," replied Mrs. Vinton; "there is but one drawback on our happiness; that is the continued absence of poor Charles."

Mr. Vinton's countenance fell immediately. "Ah, well!" he sighed; "we shall never see him again!"

"I do not despair of his return," quietly remarked Lucy.

"Could you forgive him the past if he should return, my dear husband?" anxiously queried Mrs. Vinton. "He may be kept away by fearing you would not receive him home, if he should return."

"Pshaw! pshaw!" impatiently replied Mr. Vinton; "it ill becomes us at our age to talk of not forgiving any one—particularly one of our own blood. I was perhaps too strenuous in wishing Charles to be a lawyer, he was too mulish in his opposition—but it is all over now."

"I think Charles would join us in our party to-day, if he were assured of your forgiveness."

"What! Charles—what do you say?"

"Charles is in the parlor," said Mrs. Vinton, deeply affected, "waiting your forgiveness."

"*What!* are you tricking? I see it now!"

"No, no," said Lucy, seizing him with both hands, "no, no; solemnly, truly, it is as we say."

Leaving the table, Mr. Vinton made his way to the parlor, the door was opened, was held thus a moment, then violently closed, and presently a sound like hysterical weeping came to the breakfast room. Both rushed to the parlor, and there stood the old gray-headed man with his manly son in his embrace, answering that son's petitions for pardon, by "lifting up his voice and weeping aloud."

"He is asking forgiveness of me," cried the old man," when it is I who should ask his."

"No, no," interrupted the son; "I should have submitted with a better grace to your authority."

"Well, well," interrupted the father; "we will not quarrel as to who is the greatest sinner; on that point we will agree to disagree."

And then there came a second edition of the last night's histories — a rehearsal of all the dangers, adventures and fortunes of our hero, which we will not repeat.

And now, by and by, in carryalls, barouches, chaises, and light wagons, for though it was Christmas, there was no sleighing — the company was brought to the door of the Vintons. Great was the astonishment of Emily's husband, and the indignation of her children to see her spring into the open arms of a tall, moustached, be-

whiskered, foreign-looking gentleman, whom
she threatened to suffocate with kisses. But
the astonishment of one, and the indignation
of the other were changed into the most
boisterous joy, as she released herself from
his vice-like embrace, and presented him to
her husband as her "long-absent brother
Charles," and "the dear good uncle whom
the children had never seen." And then,
when uncles, aunts, cousins and friends
poured in, not knowing the arrival of
Charles, how the Vintons re-echoed their
"wish you a merry Christmas," and then
laughed and wept, and wept and laughed, to
see how raptuously Charles was welcomed.
Evermore the tide of joy swelled higher and
higher in the house, till it seemed as if the
dwelling could not hold it. The old people
seemed to have renewed their youth, and the
young people were almost delirious with happiness; while Charles several times protested
that he would certainly have obtained an
insurance on his life, if he had supposed he
was going to fall into such violent hands.

Evening came; the Christmas tree was
lighted; and after the young folks had sufficiently admired its sparkling branches, laden
with gifts, and danced around it till they

were weary, its bountiful fruit was harvested
by them to the complete intoxication of their
little hearts. There was but one cause of
complaint among them, but on that one they
were unanimous. "Uncle Charles," who had
become a prodigious favorite among them,
"Uncle Charles had no present, although he
had been gone fifteen years, while nearly all
the rest had; this they called a great shame."

"By heavens!" said old Mr. Vinton, "'t is
a shame! He shall not be cheated out of a
Christmas gift, though; for if you can get
nothing else, you shall have Lucy," putting
the trembling, blushing girl into his arms;
"take her and keep her, and she'll be worth
more to you than all the gold and silver
you've brought from South America. There,
my boy, you can't say your father never
made you a present."

Oh, how this delighted the children!
"May n't we give three cheers for Uncle
Charles and Aunt Lucy, grandfather?" asked
one of the boys. "Don't you call *this* a merry Christmas, Uncle Charles?" said another.
"Won't you have a Christmas party every
year, grandma?" softly inquired a little girl.

"No cheering yet, boys!" interposed Mr.
Vinton; "wait a moment. I want to invite

all who are here to-day, to be present a week
from to-day, at New Year's—not a word
Charles—when we are to have a wedding.
A week is long enough for your preparations, by heavens! especially when you have
been anticipating the "happy day" for fifteen
years—hey, Lucy?" But Lucy was weeping on Charles' bosom. "And now, boys,
cheer if you want to. Hurrah!"

Three cheers were given by the crazy little fellows, good night kisses exchanged all
around, and then, happy in the day they had
spent, and happy in anticipation of the coming New Year's festival, the joyous party
broke up, unanimous in declaring this the
"merriest Christmas they had ever passed."

THE RACE WITH THE MILL STREAM.

Rain! rain! rain! It seemed as if the very "windows of heaven" were opened for a second deluge; as if the clouds would never cease emptying themselves upon the earth; as if the light of sun, moon and stars was utterly quenched by the floods. For two, three, four days, had the big rain come down, peltingly, pitilessly, ceaselessly, day and night—at times, almost like a water-spout—until the accumulated snows of winter, that were piled high in the forest, and lay deep on field and meadow, were wholly dissolved, swelling tiny streams, till they burst their icy fetters, and submerged the lands on either side of them, gullying the roads by the rivulets formed of the melting snows and the fast-falling rain, and deepening, widening, and adding volume to the mill-stream, that went roaring, rushing, and foaming through the valley, like a cataract. Still the rain poured down as remorselessly as ever; no gleam of light in the western horizon gave faint promise of fair weather; not the least break in the clouds was visible; and though it was the fourth day of the storm, one would have judged, from appearances, it had but just commenced.

Regardless of the torrents still pouring down, William Preston rose from the breakfast table, and began to equip himself for a ride to the village, two miles distant. It was Monday morning, and William always bade adieu to his little family, on that morning, for the week, as he found employment in the upper village, which could not be obtained nearer. But his gentle wife regarded his preparations with a troubled eye, and at last offered a remonstrance to his departure in the woful storm still raging.

"Why don't you wait a little, William? I am sure the rain will slack before long; it can't pour down in this way much longer."

"That's what you have been saying, these three days, Mary! But I am neither sugar nor salt; and as my work will not go on while I am here, I may as well be off, rain or shine."

"But you will be drenched to the skin, William!"

"Oh, I don't mind a drenching! I am used to it. If the rain does n't cease before long, however, we shall be drowned out here in the valley. All the meadows are under water now."

"Are you afraid of a freshet?"

"Yes—no—or, in fact, there is one already. Our house is the lowest in the valley, and the only one in danger from a freshet; and, Mary," he continued, turning from the window to his wife, buttoning his dreadnought coat to the very chin, and donning a tarpaulin of the dimensions of a a small umbrella, "if you see the water rising, and feel any fear, you had better take the children, and go higher up, to some of the neighbors—to your sister's, perhaps. And now, good morning; I am going up on horseback this morning, and shall not come in again after I have saddled Jack." And, tenderly kissing his wife, he stooped to press his lips to the brow of his little son, still sitting at the breakfast table; and yet lower, to the velvet cheek of his infant daughter, slumbering in her cradle, when he turned and left the house.

But after he had saddled his horse, and even mounted him, an uneasy feeling, that

he could not define or account for, prompted
him to ride to the door, to repeat the advice
he had given his wife but a moment before.
"Mary," he reiterated, "if it rains in this
way much longer, there will certainly be a
great freshet; the stream is up very high
now, and you must keep a sharp look-out;
and if the water comes up even to the foot
of the garden, don't delay a moment longer
—leave the house and go somewhere else.
So, good morning again; I may be home
before Saturday night, this week." And,
turning his horse's head to the village, he
drove rapidly thither, and was soon out of
sight.

All that day, and during most of the night
the rain continued to fall; and William Preston thought of his wife and children, with
inexpressible anxiety. Their house was a
frail and somewhat dilapidated structure,
that stood down low in the valley, on the
bank of the mill-stream, now converted into
a roaring river; while on either side the hills
swelled up steeply, dotted here and there,
and at last crowned with dwellings. The
channel of the stream, at this particular
point, was somewhat narrow; and as the
water was rapidly rising, and would not

subside, but rather continue to rise, for two or three days, the apprehensions of the anxious husband and father, that his family were in danger from the unusual freshet, were well founded.

The day following, he became acquainted with another fact, that revealed to him the peril of their situation more plainly.

The stream that ran through the valley, of which we have before spoken, beside which stood their dwelling, furnished the motive power to factories, saw and grist mills and machine-shops, located at convenient distances along its course. During the drought of summer, when the stream became low, the supply of water failed; and for a month or six weeks, and sometimes longer, these establishments were obliged to suspend their operations; and many poor people, who could ill afford to be idle, were thus temporarily deprived of employment. To obviate this difficulty, manufacturers, millers and machinists, had clubbed together, and, at an expense of some thousands of dollars, had built a reservoir at the head of the stream, throwing a dam across it, and erecting embankments on either side; thus reserving the surplus water for a season of drought and

need. Ordinarily, there was an immense
and powerful body of water detained here,
which extended over some fifty or seventy-
five acres of surface; but now, when over-
flowing brooks, streams and rivulets, were
pouring in their tribute to the reservoir, already swelled to a lake by the heavy rains,
it presented a most formidable appearance,
extending far and wide, dashing and rolling
its billows like a sea, committing sad depre-
dations among fences and stone walls, roads
and fields, and pouring a volume of water
over the dam whose roar could be heard at
a great distance, and causing the earth to
vibrate with the shock, in its immediate
vicinity.

The reservoir had been built in the fall,
and was not completed till winter had set
in; and, not expecting the strength of the
dam would be so severely tested, an old
flume had been put in. But it was now
feared that the dam and embankments would
prove inadequate to the vast pressure of
water against them; and a large concourse
of the villagers gathered around, watching
the roaring, surging tide, and indulging the
most painful apprehensions. If the dam
were carried away, incalculable damage

10*

would ensue to all the work-shops and man-
ufactories on the stream below; while all
who were acquainted with the peculiar location of William Preston's house hesitated
not to express their conviction that it would
be swept away like a mere toy. But the
storm had ceased, a brisk wind was blowing,
the probabilities of an accident were no
more alarming than they had been for two
days; and as night closed in upon the gos-
sipping lookers-on, they one by one retired
to their homes and beds, with a feeling of
perfect security.

No so, however, William Preston. Though
he sought his pillow, vainly did he woo the
sweet influences of sleep; he was restless
and nervous, and tormented with an indefin-
able dread of coming evil, that imparted
such acuteness to his senses that the least
sound rang upon his ears like the blast of a
trumpet, starting him from his pillow, and
thrilling him with a vague but terrible fear.
Again and again did he reproach himself for
leaving his little family in such imminent
peril, and resolve at the very earliest dawn
to return and remove them to a place of
safety; and then, as if he had administered
a sedative to his fears, he would seek to

compose himself to sleep; but in vain—no
slumber could be coaxed to his eyes. Vexed
and wearied, he rose, at last, and, half dress-
ing himself, began to pace the room, occasionally pausing to listen to the continuous
roar of the floods pouring over the dam;
when, lifting the curtain for an instant, to
look out of the window, he saw—yes, he
was not mistaken—he saw the water lying
in the front yard, up to the very door-stone!
There could be no delusion, for he plainly
saw that the stars overhead, which had come
out thickly and brightly, were mirrored from
its surface.

In an instant, he had flung on the remain-
der of his apparel, and rushed down stairs
to the door, where he could view the dam;
when he perceived that the fears of the villagers were to be realized—a portion of the
embankment was already carried away, and
it was evident that the whole, with the dam,
would soon yield to the powerful rush and
pressure of the water. It was but the work
of an instant for him to arouse the inmates
of his boarding-house, and of the dwellings
adjacent; and despatching a man to the factory, with orders to ring the alarm-bell, he
dashed into the stable, saddled his horse with

incredible celerity, mounted him, and spurred down the valley by the river course, like
one mad.

In a few moments, all was bustle, hurry
and confusion, in the village; every dwelling
in dangerous proximity to the cause of all
this terror was deserted, and women, children, and valuables were conveyed to places
of safety; horsemen were despatched round
the upper road to warn the villagers below
of the approach of the water, and one or
two bold men leaped into the saddle, and
followed in William Preston's steps ; for
they remembered the dangerous location of
his dwelling, and feared lest the mill-stream
would reach his family before him.

Cursing his tardiness in seeking safety for
his wife and little ones, and groaning aloud
at the danger that menaced them, Preston
cheered on his good steed till he sped over
the ground as if wings were added to him.
He had not proceeded one fourth of the way
when he heard an increased roar,—a dashing, rushing sound,—and screams and shouts
that rose above the deafening crash of the
dam, and the plunge of the floods; and he
knew that the dam and embankments were
carried away, and that an avalanche of wa-

ter was hurled down into the stream and upon the valley. Glancing down into the river, beside which he was riding, he saw, by the faint starlight, that its current had received a new impetus, that its volume was sensibly increased, while wreaths of white foam were dashing down its surface.

"God of heaven—help! help!" was the ejaculation that burst from the heart and lips of the agonized man; and, leaning forward to urge his horse to yet greater speed, the big drops of anguish fell from his brow upon the animal's mane, while a deadlier faintness than that of sickness seized his heart. Almost lying upon the neck of his steed, with the reins loose and flying, he spurred him on, and encouraged him to yet greater exertions; and the noble beast, as though comprehending the cause of his master's furious haste, and sympathizing in his agony, glanced furtively down upon the wild waters rushing past him, and quickened his already lightning-like speed.

Three factories lay between the upper village and William Preston's house; and scarcely had he passed the first, when the tumbling floods were down upon its dam, sweeping it away like stubble, and timbers, planks and wood came surging along on the top of the waves, that strode mercilessly down the valley, gloating. over the destruction they wrought. On they came, like an infuriated populace, leaping and tumbling, and clapping their hands in demoniac glee — and the dam of the second factory yielded to their fierce assault. On they rushed — the victorious waters — with increased force and volume, and like the very spirit of mischief, seemed hurrying to destroy the poor dwelling of the husband and father, who was running this fearful race with the waves, not for his own life, but for the lives of those dearer to him than his own.

On he flew, in the darkness — on, like the wind! Now the road was low and overflowed — and now it wound up higher, and he could look down upon the dreadful current, that threatened destruction to those so dear to him. At last — oh, what an eternity did it seem to him since he started! — he came within sight of his dwelling; all was still and quiet; its inmates evidently were not alarmed. How eagerly William Preston strained his eyes in that direction! A bright thought darted into his mind, and for an instant his heart grew lighter. "Perhaps," he said to himself, "Mary was alarmed, and went to her sister's to pass the night. Oh, heaven, I thank thee!" But no—he looked again—the faint light of the night-lamp streamed from her bedroom window; she was still there, in danger, and unconscious! As the frantic man saw the dim lamplight, he goaded on his already flying beast; and, rising in his saddle, he shouted, like one mad: "Mary! Mary! for God's sake, wake! bestir yourself! you're lost! *you're lost!* YOU'RE LOST!" But his shouts were drowned by the din of the waters that were pressing on his footsteps. The poor man looked back over his shoulder, and saw a mountain of white waves leaping down into the valley; and, like a pack of hungry wolves, they seemed yawning to devour the dear ones he was hastening to rescue. The dam of the last factory was gone, and the remorseless element, with accumulation of force and volume, was just upon the little cottage and its slumbering inmates.

But William Preston was also within a few rods of his house; his horse, white with foam, blood spurting from his nostrils, was not to be distanced even by the reinless, bridleless, hungry waves. A few more mad,

wild plunges, and he gained the front gate;
a word from his master, and the low fence
was cleared, and they stood, the horse and
his rider, at the door. With one thrust of
his foot, one heavy throw of his athletic form
against the door, it fell in, and he flew to his
wife's room. A few words, and, more than
all, his wild, frenzied looks, told the story, —
"Up, Mary! up, for the love of heaven!
quick! quick! there's no time to lose; the
dam is swept by the board, and the house is
going!" Catching the boy in his arms, while
the mother folded the babe to her bosom,
. they hurried from the doomed cottage, into
which the waves were beginning to enter; —
partly leaping, partly lifted, Mary was seated
in the saddle, and seizing the horse by the
bridle, while both master and animal rallied
their exhausted strength for a last effort,
they climbed up the steep bank to the first
dwelling, and looked back to see the white
floods pouring in at the doors and windows
of their deserted home.

"Thank God! thank God, Mary, you're
safe! you're safe! Knock at the door, and
arouse the folks; for it is all dark around
me—I cannot see my way!" and the voice
of the overtaxed man died away, and he

sank upon the ground, in a protracted swoon.

But the men who had followed him from the village were soon with him, and shelter and every comfort was bestowed upon his wife and children that their circumstances demanded. An attempt was made to save some of the household stuff from the watery element; but the waves were waging so violent a war upon the dwelling, that it was abandoned as hazardous and impracticable. When the morning dawned, a broad river rolled through the valley, while not a vestige of William Preston's house was visible.

"I have run races, in my lifetime, often," William Preston would say, when concluding the story we have related—"I have run races on foot, when a boy, with my playmates, for marbles, a hoop, or an apple; and I have raced on horseback, when a man, for a purse of money; but the toughest, most exciting, and wildest race I ever ran in my life, was the RACE WITH THE MILL-STREAM, for my wife and children."

"Afflictions are frequently blessings in disguise." How many, many times, when a school-girl, have I written this sentence on the page of my blue covered copy-book, vainly endeavoring to imitate the beautiful chirography of the copper-plate "slip," and sorely puzzling my poor brain, all the while, to comprehend the meaning of the contradictory assertion. Had the sentence been "Bitter is sweet," or "Light is darkness," it would have been quite as intelligible to me, and equally as sensible—for had not my eight years' experience in human affairs acquainted me with afflictions? Had I not sometimes lost my place in my class, seen a favorite kitten die, had a fit of the tooth-ache, or been sent to bed before dark as a punishment? If *these* were not afflictions, what were? And had I not sense enough to know that they were very far from being blessings? Certainly. It was, therefore,

speedily settled in my young mind, that not
only the above aphorism, but another very
like it, which we find in the Holy Book,—
"It is good for me to be afflicted,"—was
wholly devoid of common sense.

Ah, how vastly different from this, is the
lesson time has taught me! How emphati-
cally true have I since found the utterance
of the beautiful Swedish authoress—"Suffering is the plough which turns up the field of
the soul, into whose deep furrows the All-
wise Husbandman scatters his heavenly
seed." How often have I seen the heart in-
toxicated with prosperity; made capricious
by kindness, and tainted with selfishness by
years of unalloyed happiness, regenerated
through the discipline of sorrow! How
many have come forth from the fiery ordeal
of intense suffering; purified from the dross,
that before mingled largely with the nobler
elements of their nature! Yes, the mission
of sorrow *is* beneficent, could we always understand it aright!

When I was some seven or eight years of
age, I was transferred from one of the "Pri-
mary schools" of good old Boston, where,
among other juveniles, I had learned to read,
spell, and repeat the multiplication table, to

one of the "Grammar schools" of the city, where were ten hundred or more pupils, of ages varying from six to sixteen. I well remember the day of my debut at the ―― school. The vastness of the school-room, which to my ignorance and inexperience, seemed almost immeasurable, the varied figures and faces of its occupants, the multiplicity of their employments, the decided, peremptory tones of the teachers, the marshaling of classes for recitation, and the clock-like regularity that characterized all movements and operations—all this was very imposing to my youthful imagination, and filled me with fear and gladness—gladness, that my little stage of action had become enlarged, and fear, lest amid this multitude of strangers, I should fail to find as loving playmates, as had been mine in the junior department from which I was just emancipated. But all other impressions were faint, in comparison with that made upon my fancy, by a singularly beautiful girl, about fourteen years of age. On that first day, as often as my eye roved over the sea of faces around me, it finally settled with satisfaction upon that one beautiful girl— beautiful, superlatively, even among the many beaming faces of childhood and dawning womanhood that clustered around her. If she walked from her seat, my eye followed her graceful figure, as one might gaze on the movements of a vanishing angel; and if she smiled, I felt my heart dance in my bosom for very gladness. School was dismissed, and then I saw groups of her classmates fluttering around her,—for none are more ardent admirers of the beautiful than children,—and I soon learned by the words of endearment addressed to her, that she inspired not only admiration, but affection.

Days passed away, and I neglected no opportunity of feasting my eyes upon the fascinations of the beautiful girl, Augusta Lovell, for so they called her. Children are quick-sighted—and I was not long in perceiving that the little beauty was a great favorite with the teachers, although by no means as prompt at the recitations, or as observant of the regulations of our miniature, community, as many others. Twenty times a day, I would hear her name pronounced by the sonorous voice of the teacher, coupled with the injunction, "Study!" and scarcely a day passed that some offence was not charged against her—and yet, though not a

studious pupil, and constantly doing wrong,
her misdemeanors, and non-recitations were
rarely visited by the penalties inflicted on
other offenders. Everything that I knew of
her during her attendance at school, would
go to prove Augusta Lovell indolent, except
at play, unstable, and thoughtless in all
things—but heaven had fashioned her most
beautiful, she was endowed with an affectionate nature, was irresistibly witching in all
her moods, fascinating in her manners—and
her failings were almost entirely overlooked.

If she hesitated at a recitation, a dozen of
her mates were ready to run the risk of punishment, by acting as her prompters; and
that, too, when her failure would elevate
them in the class; if a monitor was station-
ed to report those, who, slyly or openly,
dared be guilty of breaches of decorum,
though she frolicked till her merriment attracted the attention of the Principal, and
. threw a whole class into disorder, and
though she ran from her seat every other
moment without the necessary permission—
the partial sentinel had neither eyes nor ears
for her venturesome feats.

Augusta's life, even while at school, was
one continued gala-day. Almost daily, dur-

ing the season of festivities, she came to
school, with her wealth of bright hair that
could hardly be kept from curling at any
rate, rolled up in papers, that the glittering
ringlets might be brighter and fresher than
usual—a sure indication with us, in those
days, that the head thus attired, was bound
for a party in the evening. If we went upon
an excursion—sleighing, sailing or picnic-
ing—innumerable were the beaux that strove
for the honor of serving the fair Augusta,
while the rest of us, poor things! were left
to look out for ourselves.

By and by, after I had been a year at the
—— school, Augusta left it; and for a few
days, the school-room seemed dark to me, as
if the sunshine were shut out from it. I was
too young to have formed an acquaintance
with the heroine of my narrative, even had
other circumstances favored it—but I often
thought of her, and wondered if she were as
singularly beautiful and fascinating as ever.
I was therefore right glad, when, half a doz-
en years after, she was thrown once more
within my sphere of observation. She was
then in the full bloom of beauty—a being
of surpassing, and I might say in truth, of
dazzling loveliness. Her life was gliding on

11

like a dream of fairy-land, no sorrow invaded it—no dark cloud shadowed it—no trial was known to her—and it seemed that she was to be spoiled for a lack of that dreaded adversity, which chastens, while it strengthens and disciplines the character. Idolized by her relatives, living in the midst of the gaieties of a brilliant city circle, receiving the universal admiration meted out to her, the gay cynosure of all eyes, the reigning queen of "belle-dom," it is not strange that one of her indolent and thoughtless nature should have become volatile and vain, and quite unfitted for the duties and realities of this stern world. Underlaying the vanity, frivolity and thoughtlessness, but too apparent to the most superficial observer of character, there were in Augusta's nature, as high and noble faculties as ever swelled the heart of woman; but they had never yet been called forth, no opportunity had ever arisen for their exercise, and the magic power was yet to be developed, which should wake them into active life.

The twenty-first birthday of Augusta was an important day to her, for it was her bridal day; and to both of the wedded parties, it came freighted with happiness and bright

promises. The world, with its usual freedom of comment, pronounced the union a
"strange match," and spake of the wedded
ones as an "ill-assorted couple!" though it
was not stranger, or more ill-assorted, than
are dozens of marriages that occur about us
every day. Mr. Loring was, perhaps, ten
years older than his bride, and possessed a
character just the reverse of hers. In the
same proportion as she was volatile, unstable, thoughtless and inconsiderate, he was
sedate, serious, reflecting and decided. Once
drawn within the magic circle of Augusta's
influence, he could but accord to her what
every one else yielded — admiration and
affection. Despite her failings, it was impossible not to love her; for her nature was
so deeply affectionate, and her manners so
winning, that the severest censor would soon
forget his strictures in the drawing out of
his heart towards her.

Augusta's marriage threw open to her yet
wider the halls of pleasure. Her husband
was wealthy, and every means of enjoyment
furnished by riches, was therefore placed in
her power; society meted out to her its homage with a more prodigal hand, the votaries
of fashion led her through the gay round of

11K

fashionable pleasures, and initiated her into the mysteries of fashionable dissipation; and before the first year of their marriage closed, Mr. Loring saw with pain, that his wife was living only for pleasure, and that domestic life had not for her the charms it had for him.

The birth of a beautiful boy checked for a time Augusta's dissipated career, and Mr. Loring rejoiced over what he deemed the awakening of his wife's better and nobler nature. The novelty of being a mother, of holding in her arms, and pressing to her heart her little one, wholly occupied her thoughts for a season, and diverted her attention from the gay scenes in which, since her marriage, she had mingled. But the novelty was soon gone, and though the mother really loved her child, yet she longed again for the exhilaration of the evening soiree, the assembly-room and theater, and so gave her babe to the care of a hireling nurse, who, she would fain have persuaded herself, knew better how to manage it than herself. Mr. Loring protested gently and kindly against this unnatural course, but his beautiful wife, unused to words of disapprobation, lifted to his, her eyes suffused with tears, and he asked forgiveness. Still he was dissatisfied — and when he saw that the thoughtless, giddy mother soon became a comparative stranger to her child, he resolved to atone to the neglected boy, for his mother's lack of attention, by his own devotion.

A second child was given them, a little girl; but though Mrs. Loring seemed pleased with the helpless little stranger, its birth made less impression on her heart and mind, than did that of her first-born, and a few weeks saw her again in the brilliant halls of fashion. Mr. Loring now became seriously alarmed at his wife's course, at her neglect of home and its duties, and at the eagerness with which she plunged into the vortex of fashionable city life; and he sought to draw her from the giddy whirl of fashion through which she was borne. He was met in his efforts by tears and remonstrances; by palliations of her conduct, and reference to the precedent established by others, who had inducted her into her present mode of life; and finding that her heart was set on the gaieties to which she had become accustomed, and having no inclination for domestic warfare, he forbore farther entreaty, and trusted to time and circumstance to effect the change he so much desired.

Eight years sped away—but they witnessed no change for the better in the life of
Mrs. Loring.   Four children called her
mother; but their claims on her time and
attention were not allowed, and she was as
little confined to her home by cares and
responsibilities, as little debarred from the
pleasures of gay life, as in the freest days
of her maidenhood.   Her husband had long
ceased expostulation or comment on her frivolity, and had left her free and unchecked
to gratify her peculiar tastes and inclinations.
He had wholly withdrawn from the gay
world, for he had resolved to supply to his
children their lack of a mother's care and
attention; and every moment of leisure afforded by his business was devoted to his
little ones.   While his wife was hurrying,
evening after evening, from soiree to soiree,
his hours were spent with his children, to
whom his affectionate and judicious converse, his sympathy and counsel, and his
superintendence of their education were of
incalculable benefit.   Of his wife, he saw but
little, for he rarely accompanied her to the
festivities upon which she lavished time and
money most prodigally: and had not the
giddy wife been blinded by "the god of this

world," she would have noticed the paleness and sorrow that at last became habitual to his face, at this divorce of their employments and interests. But she never lacked for attendants, gayer, more humorsome, and less serious than her husband; and she soon ceased to deprecate, even in words, his "lack of gallantry," and became even pleased with the exchange.

Alas for poor Augusta! she little knew the whispered remarks that passed from one to another, as each evening witnessed her presence at the resorts of the pleasure-seeking, unattended by him who should have been her guide and companion! She little knew the calumnies uttered by the tongue of scandal, as she approached, hanging upon the arm of one or another of those "men of fashion," whom, a few years before, she would have shunned as she would a viper! Had she known the epithets coupled with her name by those who beheld her nightly flirtations with men, whose hearts were festering with moral corruption, it would surely have forced her into the right and safe path. Poor Augusta! it was a dark time for her, though she knew it not. But a step was between her and irretrievable ruin; but a

step between her and the entire forfeiture
of her husband's regard, and separation from
both husband and children.   Would not
any instrumentality be merciful that averted the impending ruin—that awoke her to
right and duty?   The physician amputates
a limb that he may save the patient—he
probes to the living flesh the gangrenous
wound for the healing of the system—and
we bless him, we tender to him our thanks.
Oh, should we not much more then, bless the
great Physician of souls, who chasteneth for
our own good, and buries the arrows of affliction deep in the quivering heart, for the sal-
vation of the whole moral nature?

The clock had struck two of the morning,
when Augusta Loring alighted from her carriage, and hurried through the hall, and over
the stairs, to her apartment.   Here she found
her husband waiting for her—an unusual
occurrence, for his hours of retiring and rising varied much from those observed by his
wife, who started with surprise, at seeing
him.

"Why, William! up yet?"

He bowed seriously, and Mrs. Loring, re-
garding him more earnestly, noticed what
others had long perceived, that he was pale

-and thin. Alarmed, she sprang forward, and laying her hand on his shoulder, and looking into his face, asked, in agitation,—

"What is the matter? Are you ill?"

"No."

"Could n't you sleep?"

"I have not tried."

"What has kept you up so late, pray?"

"I wanted to see you, and did not know as I should have another opportunity than the present."

"Heavens, William! what *do* you mean? You frighten me out of my wits."

"There is no cause of alarm, Augusta; lay off your hat and shawl, and come and sit here."

Mrs. Loring did as her husband desired, and having dismissed her maid to her bed, sat down beside him, pale with vague fear, and trembling with apprehension.

Sorrowfully, Mr. Loring turned towards her. "I have unpleasant news for you, Augusta, which I have deferred communicating until the last moment."

Mrs. Loring trembled violently from head to foot, and fixed her eyes on her husband with painful earnestness. There was something in his calm, sorrowful face, that reproached and alarmed her, more than his words.

"My business requires my absence from home, for awhile, and to-morrow I sail for New Orleans."

"William!"

"I have tried to make some other arrangement, for the children need my attention very much—but I cannot. I do not know what will become of *them* in my absence."

This indirect but deserved reproach went to the heart of Mrs. Loring, whose feelings were now wrought to a high pitch of excitement, and bursting into tears, she sobbed on her husband's shoulder. Affectionately, as though she had been to him and his children all that a wife and mother should be, he put his arm around her, and soothed her with kind words. He was to be absent for a year; for from New Orleans he was to proceed to Liverpool and Paris, and he unfolded to his wife his whole plan. "And now, Augusta," he added in conclusion, "let me say to you, that I tremble, when I think of our children during the coming year. What can reasonably be expected of them, if they are given wholly to the care of hired women? You have found pleasure in the round of gaieties, to which we have been invited; and that you might enjoy uninterruptedly your pleasures, I have endeavored to supply your place to the dear children. But what will become of them while I am away? I am torn with anxiety about them."

"William," said the weeping wife, raising her head from her husband's shoulder, and speaking earnestly, "I have done wrong; I have done wrong! Why did you leave me so wholly to myself? How can you forgive me, when I have been so neglectful? How can you ever again love me?" And burying her face again on his shoulder, she wept afresh.

"Do not reproach yourself, Augusta," was the reply. "I have always known you were right at heart, only you have become somewhat bewildered by the giddy life you have led. But I am sure you will care for the children when I am away, and will attend to them as I have?"

"I will! I will, certainly, William!"

"You will find it a delightful task! If sickness comes to them, while I am away, if death, let a mother's care and tenderness be theirs; if I feel assured of this, I shall part with you all the more easily."

Never before had Mr. Loring seemed so good and so dear to his wife, as now, and never had she seemed to herself so unpardonably culpable in her neglect of him. She accompanied him to the nursery, where slept her babes, and there, while she bedewed their round, rosy faces with her tears, and wondered how she could have held herself so aloof from them, and mourned over her cruel indifference to them, she promised in language, and with a manner that left no doubt of her sincerity and good intentions, to cherish them during his absence most tenderly.

Mr. Loring's heart overflowed — not a word of censure did he utter, not a doubt but that her promise would be kept in good faith, but bestowing upon the penitent and tearful wife those little endearments that come to us so gratefully from those we love, he sought to strengthen her good resolution by words of cheer and encouragement. And when, on the next day, he bade "good by" to the sorrowing little group composed of his household, it was with a heart at rest, and full of love for them all, not excepting her, whose every fault was obliterated from his memory by her tears, repentance and promises of the few hours before.

And did Augusta Loring remember her penitence, her husband's request, and her promise? Yes, for a time. Weeks after his departure, attention was given so closely and untiringly to her children, that their father's absence was almost unnoted by them. Her first morning duty was connected with them, and her last before retiring, was to kiss them "good night," as they lay slumbering on their pillows. For their sakes, and for his, who was far away, she renounced temporarily the gaieties which had heretofore so deeply engrossed her; and in her inmost heart vowed henceforth to be as domestic and home-loving as her husband would have her. Fifty times a day she congratulated herself on her amendment, and thanked heaven that the honied speeches and flattering attentions of her butterfly attendants, and her reception of them, was unknown to her husband, who had now become inexpressibly dear to her. With rapture, she anticipated the hour of his return, when he would shower upon her affectionate commendations, which the children would cause to be redoubled, by their little tales of their mother's faithfulness and tenderness. And then her face would crimson with pleasure, the tears would start to her eyes, and she would say, "Dear William! it is, as he said, pleasanter to do right than wrong!"

But alas for poor human nature! Mrs. Loring was not yet as strong as she imagined, nor as able to cope with temptation. An invitation to a grand fancy ball, the first of the season, was the first serious temptation thrown in her way, and the first event which at all inclined her to deviate from her good resolutions. At first she said, "No, her husband was absent, the care of her children would prevent," and so on, but one and another of her fashionable friends urged her attendance, declared it a shame for one so young and beautiful to mope herself to death because her husband was from home; and in short, by dint of flattery, coaxing, sarcasm and persuasion, her scruples were overcome, and she consented to grace the festal occasion with her presence. "It is only for this once," she said, and so she intended; but it proved otherwise; and this ball, which was the first of a series, was the first step to a retrograde movement that carried poor Augusta back deeper into dissipation than ever. Again were her children neglected, the hours consumed in revelry, dress, fashion, and gay society, and to elicit admiration was again the object of her existence

"One would suppose Mrs. Loring unmarried," was the frequent remark of those who witnessed her wild gaiety, her reckless flirtations, and her apparent forgetfulness of husband and children — and when it became known that one of her admirers was a constant hanger-on at her house, her exclusive companion in her rides and promenades, at balls, concerts, soirees, dinner-parties and other like places, that his admiration was undisguised, his affection apparent, out-spoken and allowed, many said, "It is a great pity that Mrs. Loring is *not* unmarried."

Scandalous reports began to circulate freely, the wrong of which Augusta was guilty, was a thousand fold magnified, and many a mother looked aghast at her, and prayed heaven their daughters might never sink so low. Some, however, more friendly and less malicious, believing her to be merely imprudent and not criminal, which was the truth, sought an interview with the giddy woman, detailed to her the gossiping reports in circulation concerning her, and begged of her to act with more circumspection. This, in conjunction with a letter received at the same

time from her husband, announcing his prob-
able return in the next steamer, produced
some effect, and again the unstable Augusta
was sunk in the depths of penitence, writh-
ing under the agonies of remorse and in-
wardly promising amendment.

The day at last arrived — the steamer was
telegraphed, and then the boom of the signal gun announced her arrival. Mrs. Loring
sprang from her bed as these long looked-for
signals came to her ear, and making her toilet more rapidly than ever before, she hurried
to the nursery to awake the little ones.

"Papa will be here soon," she said to
them, "and you must be up and dressed
nicely when he comes," — and the happy,
light-hearted beings bounded from their pillows, and soon filled the house with their
glee, and shouts of "papa's coming! papa's
coming!"

No heart of that little company beat more
happily than the mother's; for though conscious of having failed in duty to her children, of having neglected her promise, and
brought dishonor upon herself and husband,
and in the estimation of many of her friends,
yet she had resolved to confess all to him on
his return, to renew again her promises, and

to put herself completely under his judicious guidance — and she knew his fond heart too well to doubt the result would be in her favor.

But though her heart almost leaped from her bosom whenever the sound of carriage wheels approached the house, yet the hours of the early morning wore away, and still he came not. Impatience began to consume her, and half fearing that something had prevented his return at the intended time, she ordered the carriage, and directed the coachman to drive rapidly to the —— wharf. As the coach was dashing along the streets, the eye of Mrs. Loring was caught by Mr. Bond, her husband's partner in business, who was walking in an opposite direction, but who, on perceiving her, made a movement towards the carriage, as if he would speak with her. She instantly pulled the check-string, but Mr. Bond had already given the coachman a signal to stop, and the horses were speedily reined up to the sidewalk where that gentleman was standing.

"You were going to the steamer to meet Mr. Loring," was his remark, after the usual salutations were over, "were you not?"

Mrs. Loring replied in the affirmative, and

12

eagerly inquired "if her husband had arrived?"

"He is confidently expected," was the evasive answer, "and by a letter, I learned had spoken his passage in this steamer; but my dear madam, there is always a great crowd collected at the wharf—a perfect mob—so that it is a very unpleasant place to meet friends, hardly fitting for a lady. Would Mr. Loring desire you to meet him there—would he think it proper?"

Mrs. Loring colored, and looked confused. She had been so much censured of late, that she had lost confidence in herself, and had grown timid. Before she could frame any reply, Mr. Bond spoke again: "Allow me to give orders to your coachman to drive home again; that will be the better course, and I will accompany you thither;" and without waiting her consent, the order was given, and the horses' heads were turned towards her dwelling.

Surprised and indignant at this strange procedure, Mrs. Loring was silent; but her thoughts were busy. "Mr. Bond is beside himself to offer such impertinence," was her first thought; but then she remembered his query, "is it proper?" and she sank back in despondency. "I can never do any thing right, now-a-days; I should like to know if I *am indeed*, so ignorant and regardless of the rules of propriety, as people would make me believe!" these were her second thoughts. Mr. Bond did not appear to notice her surprise or displeasure, but chatted away on indifferent subjects, in a manner very unusual with him, until they reached the house.

As the coach stopped, and the steps were let down to alight, the door opened, and her husband's eldest brother came forward to hand her from the carriage. *His* appearance there, at that hour, seemed as strange to Mrs. Loring as Mr. Bond's interference; but she kept her thoughts to herself, and extending her hand, said jocosely, " William is not half as anxious to meet us, as we are to meet him, or he would have been here before now." An indifferent reply was given, but with a seriousness of demeanor, a sadness, it might have been, that ill accorded with the light words, and Mrs. Loring's heart began to quake with fear. She looked scrutinizingly at both gentlemen for a moment, but she could not read their faces; there was a mystery, a sadness veiling them, that she dared not explain, even to herself.

A terrible fear came over her, her limbs trembled, and her brother's assistance was needed, to enable her to reach the parlor. Here, her mother met her, who was not wont to leave home at this unusual hour of the morning, and Augusta sank down upon the sofa, the blood in her veins seeming to curdle with her increasing terror. Mrs. Lovell came towards her, and began to untie her hat, and lay off her shawl, and Mr. Bond brought a glass of water, and held it to her colorless lips; the tears of one trickled fast upon her face, and the hand of the other trembled as it supported her — but no one spoke.

Mrs. Loring understood the tears, the agitation, and the silence—she knew all! Words were not needed to inform her that the meeting with her husband would be in heaven, and not on earth!

But Mr. Loring, the brother, at last broke the painful silence. "Augusta," he asked, "when did you hear from William?"

The date of the letter was given, and her brother again inquired, "Did he say anything of his health?"

"He said he *had* been somewhat ill," replied Mrs. Loring faintly, "but was then better."

"He had been more ill than he wrote you, for his life was for some time in jeopardy from typhus fever —"

"And he is now sick in Liverpool," interrupted Mrs. Loring, as if she wished to defer the utterance of the words she dreaded to hear.

"No, he is not in Liverpool: he embarked in this steamer, but immediately from overexertion, a relapse of the fever came on; he was ill all the passage, and — and —"

Mr. Loring's voice grew husky, and tremulous. Mr. Bond rose to pace the floor, to hide his agitation, and Mrs. Lovell wept aloud.

Augusta looked steadily in her brother's face, waiting the completion of the sentence, but it came not; and sinking back, and passing her tremulous hand over her pale brow, she almost whispered, yet was distinctly heard, "and — is — now — *dead!*"

Mrs. Lovell enfolded her stricken child in her arms, and Mr. Loring sitting down beside her, took her passive hand tenderly in his, but neither of them could utter a word. There are moments when even the voice of kindness and sympathy will torture the heart, when to sit down and weep with the afflicted will be more soothing than to pour forth the language of commiseration — this was such a time. Poor Augusta was stunned by the suddenness of the blow, which had stricken her husband into the grave; she gave way to no violent out-burst of grief, to no wild lamentations, not even did she weep; but the fixedness of her countenance, and its vacuity of expression, manifested how little she could realize the tidings just broken to her. Not until informed that her husband's body was brought home by the steamer — for he had died but the day before — and that it was to be brought to his house for burial, did Mrs. Loring manifest any consciousness; and then she remarked, "I am glad of that, for I shall see him once more."

But when his coffined corse was brought before her, when she gazed on those cold, but well-known features, and listened to the wailings of her fatherless babes, then she felt the full force of her affliction, and the fountains of her grief were unsealed. Then her tears rained upon his pale face as though her "eyes were" indeed "a fountain of tears."

Weak as an infant, and almost as passive, only now and then asking a question in so

sorrowful tone of voice that it made one
weep to hear it, she was prepared for the
funeral obsequies. The usual consolations
of religion were tendered her, but the hopeless look of woe that sat on her face, the
slight moan that now and then was wrung
from her, and the intense eagerness with
which her eyes followed the coffin, told
plainly that the anguish of her spirit was not
soothed. Some wondered at her grief; for
they could not understand her sorrow, when
they remembered her late levity; and others
who sympathized, yet felt consoled by the
thought that her grief could not last long, so
volatile was her nature — but who of us can
understand the heart of another? Who can
pierce its recesses, and divine the depth of
its love or its sorrow?

The last sad rites were over, and no demand being made on Augusta for farther
effort, she sunk under the burden of 'her
grief. It soon became necessary to summon
a physician, who prescribed tonics for her
debility, anodynes for her nervous excitement, and stimulants for her failing system
— but they were unavailing, for they could
not minister to a mind diseased, they could
not heal a wounded heart. Weeks passed

away, and still they found her confined to her bed, weak, nerveless, hopeless, and emaciated.

"She must be roused from this apathetic state," said the physician, "or she will die;" but how was this to be done? Friends called to condole with her, but she shook her head when begged to admit them, and said, "They are kind to call, but I *cannot* see them!" Her children were sent to her bedside, but she heeded not their caresses, nor their tears, and only motioned them away. Relatives remonstrated with her, and prayed her, if she would save her life, to shake off the sadness which every day was chaining her more securely to her couch — but she only replied sorrowfully, "let me die! I don't want to live!" Ministers of religion spake consolingly to her, and depicting the happiness of him whom she mourned, begged her to be comforted — but she replied only by pressing her hands over her eyes, while the tears trickled down between her thin fingers. Every effort was made to break the torpor of grief in which she was steeled — but unsuccessfully.

Remorse was busy at her heart, for her neglect of him who had ever been to her all

kindness, was as vivid as an affair of yesterday. His gentle chidings, his affectionate
remonstrances, their last sad interview, her
unkindness to the dead, her broken promises,
her wounding of his feelings, her neglect of
his happiness, her devotion to others — these
were her memories of the Past — and the
Past was irretrievable! Oh, memory! what
an abyss of misery art thou! With thee, the
Past is all, there is no Present, no Future!
No wonder that hopeless despair was wasting her away! No one divined the current
of her thoughts; no one poured balm into the
deepest wound of her heart, no one offered
consolation that reached her case!

Among the papers of Mr. Loring was an
unfinished letter to his wife, dated soon after
his recovery from the fever, containing the
particulars of his illness, which, owing to a
press of business, or the fear that she would
be alarmed, was not completed. His miniature was also among his effects, superbly
encased, taken by a celebrated artist of
Paris, and evidently intended as a present to
his wife; but these had been kept from her,
thus far, from fear of the effect they might
produce. But as every means to arouse her
to life had failed, the physician advised that

these should be given into her hand; and accordingly they were placed upon her dressing-table, so that she could not fail to see them, whether raised in bed, or sitting in the arm-chair. As was expected, the next time she was lifted into the easy-chair, her eye fell on the miniature, and then on the hand-writing of her husband; and weak as she was, she sprang forward, and eagerly, and with a slight cry of joy, grasped them.

It was indeed affecting to see how the fountains of feeling were stirred to their depths by the likeness of her husband. Again and again she pressed it to her lips and heart, large tears rolled over her wan cheeks, and words of endearment came from her colorless lips. But when she read the lines his hand had traced to her, expressive of his undying affection, of the consolation imparted to him, when he thought his hour of death was nigh, by the memory of the promises she had made to be faithful to their children — promises, he doubted not that would be kept; — when she read how much happiness he hoped to find in the bosom of his family on his return, how eager he was to see her, and enjoy her society, as he had not since their marriage — when she read this, it seemed as if the spell that had so long bound her, was broken.

"Mother," she said, addressing Mrs. Lovell, "I will be worthy my husband's name and memory—I will be to his children, what he would have desired, had he spoken with me when dying. I will no longer desire to die, but for their sakes, and for his who so loved them, I will strive to live and discharge my duty. While my husband lived, I failed in my duties to my family—now that he is dead, I will atone by my devotion."

When the children came again to her room, they were received with a welcome and a tenderness that made them wild with joy — and when friends came to offer consolation, they were admitted to her presence. The greatest obstacle in the way of her restoration to health was now removed, and the skill of her physician was exerted more effectually than before. Gradually strength came to her system, and she was again able to mingle in the active scenes of life. But it was soon apparent that a change had passed over her — a change, at which the angel in heaven, from whom she had been separated, must have rejoiced, if permitted to know aught of earthly things. Sorrow had fulfilled its mission for her — it had accomplished its most beneficent work; and had purified and ennobled by its discipline, the nature, which before, possessed much that was unlovely.

Not now does the youthful matron seek her enjoyment in the glittering, but hollow world of fashion — not now does she court admiration, and honied words of flattery — not now is she reckoned as a star in the galaxy of fashionable beauty. But in the nursery, or sitting-room, with her children around her, under whose tutelage they are daily becoming wiser and better — striving to develope aright their moral natures, to impart to them instruction, or afford them amusement — in the sanctuary, where the heavenly lessons given, are, by her, gratefully received — in the dwellings of the poor, where the tongue of honest poverty blesses her, and the eye, hollow from disease smiles thankfully upon her — in the house of affliction, where is felt the value of her sympathy — there may she now be found, with her whole heart in these duties, happier than formerly, when she bowed at the shrine of pleasure and of fashion.

And though she has her hours of utter

abandonment, when the weary spirit longs for release, when with one of old, she exclaims, " 'Twere better for me to die, and not live," yet these clouds pass away from her horizon, leaving it brighter and clearer than before. And her lone journey of life is cheered by the thought, that were *he* living, whom, when living, she valued too lightly, her course of life would please him, and the path which she has marked out, would also be his — and that, though departed, he is with her when she knows it not, gazing upon her face though she may not see *him*, and following her in her routine of duties with a satisfaction that he cannot *now* express to her.

Ah, there is *meaning* in the aphorism, "Afflictions are frequently blessings in disguise!"

THE LAST JEWEL.

I have rifled my casket of jewels most rare,
I have plucked out the brilliants that flashed in my
      hair; —
I am girded no more with a cincture of light,
That blazed as if studded with stars of the night.

I have put on the sackcloth, in woe for my dead!
And my jewels — alas! I have bartered for bread!
From the depth of the casket each gem hath been
      reft
By the mandate of hunger! One only is left!

One only — the jewel with which I was wed
To thee, who art slumbering now with the dead!
One only — the jewel thou gavest in pride,
When I knelt at the altar, thy happy young bride!

'Tis the last link that holds me to days that are
      passed,
That were freighted too fully with gladness to last;
'Tis a relic of years when the months were all
      May —
When sunshine and pleasure made blissful each
      day!

'Twas a balm-breathing morn, in the earliest spring,
When he placed on my finger this pearl-studded
  ring;
In what accents of sweetness he named me his wife,
Whose being with his was now blended for life!

I saw not the cloud that stretched far up the sky;
I deemed not the angel of death was so nigh;
Four bright summers faded, and I was bereft!
The dear one who loved me was taken — I, left!

Through sorrow and sickness, through hunger and
  cold,
I ever have clung to this circlet of gold!
I cannot — *I cannot* pawn this like the rest —
For *his* love bestowed it who dwells with the blest!

But ah! heavy the pressure of poverty's hand,
And fiercer and louder is hunger's demand!
My sireless children — O God! how they weep,
And murmur for bread, in their innocent sleep!

The birds of the forest have food and to spare; —
But ye, poor little nestlings, how scanty ye fare!
God heareth the ravens when hungry they cry —
Doth the wail of my children not pierce to the sky?

Nay, dear little birdling! start not from thy sleep!
Why wak'st thou from slumber, and only to weep?
Bread — *bread* — art thou asking? — The struggle is
  past!
I will pawn the last jewel — 'tis the last! — 'tis the
  last!

I will go to the Shylock who traffics in gems,
Who would dole but a pittance for king's diadems!
Once more will I seek for the food that ye crave —
And then — and then — dear ones! — *we have but the grave!*

THE FIRST QUARREL.

"And so you think I shall not be so very happy, after all, mother, do you?" asked Anna Hastings, as she sat at her toilet, where she had been twining her fingers abstractedly through her long, rich hair, for the last few moments, at the same time sighing heavily, as though a burden lay upon her heart.

"I did not say *that*, dear, did I?" replied Mrs. Hastings, tenderly, drawing the silky tresses from the hand of her fair daughter, and beginning herself to plait them most tastefully. "I was merely trying to persuade you to build your air-castles a little less in the clouds, and rather more on terra firma. I am sure you will be happy, my dear child, if you seek happiness aright."

"But what do you mean, mother? You have often spoken as though you feared I might not be as happy as I expect to be. Is not Henry Hamilton good and affectionate, and will he not prove a good husband?"

13м

"Yes, under some circumstanoes he will be. But I fear he may meet with trials as your husband, that he has not experienced as your lover."

"What, dear mother?"

"Well, to come directly to the point, how do you think he will bear those sudden gusts of passion, those violent fits of anger, with which you please occasionally to entertain us?"

"Oh, la! mother! what a question! Why, I shall *never* get angry with Henry. I am sure *we* shall never have a jar, or a hard word."

"If I could believe so, I should feel quite at ease in relation to your future happiness."

"Is this all you have meant, while you have been talking to me so solemnly about the uncertainty of earthly happiness, and all that sort of thing? Oh, fie, dear mother!" and Anna threw back her head, and looking up to her mother's face roguishly, tapped her familiarly on the cheek.

"Ah, my dear girl, let me beg you to heed more seriously what I have said. Kindly, but candidly, Anna, I sometimes fear lest your passionate temper may yet wreck your happiness."

"Oh, no, no, dear mother! don't say that! When I am Henry Hamilton's wife, you will see how good and equable, and meek and sweet-tempered I shall become. Why, I have resolved to be a pattern wife."

"I hope you may, but fear still that the fiery spirit that sometimes leads you to wound deeply the friends you love, now, will reveal itself even after your marriage."

"Never, mother, never! I have resolved against ever getting so *very* angry, as you have sometimes seen me. But I do not get angry *very* often, do I?"

"The habit grows on you; and let me tell you, dearest, that your occasional fits of anger, and seasons of irritability, will, if indulged, soon become every-day occurrences — and they will completely destroy all the good influence you may exert over your husband in your pleasant moods. Meekness and forbearance you must learn to practise, for they are called into daily exercise in married life. This is my last conversation of the kind with you, as you leave home to-night, and so bear with your mother, as she begs you to curb your spirit, and to keep in constant subjection your temper. Henry Hamilton will not brook many angry

13

words, even from the wife of his bosom, and your very first quarrel may prove disastrous to you both."

For a moment, Anna looked serious, and thoughtful; but she was strong in self-confidence, and sanguine in her anticipations of the future, and instantly recovering her gaiety, she replied, "I shall never quarrel with him, I *know* I never shall! and I shall prove you a false prophet, my own mother, by being one of the best and happiest of wives."

Rapidly moved the fingers of Mrs. Hastings through the luxuriant hair of her child, and soon the glossy chestnut tresses were arranged for the young girl's bridal, the rest of the toilet was made, and taking the proffered arm of her betrothed, she descended to the parlor, where a large company was waiting, and in a few moments the words were pronounced that made her the wife of him to whom she had given her heart. But little time was afforded for merriment or congratulations, for the home of the wedded couple was some twenty miles distant, and as soon as possible they bade adieu to friends and relatives, and started for their new home.

It was a beautiful evening in midsummer, and the moon, just coming up from behind the hills, silvered earth, sea, and air, with her mellow light, and beautified all things, even the meanest, with her holy presence. The calmness of the evening hour, its silently descending dews, its balmy air, on which thousands of wild flowers had flung their fragrance; the merry dancing of the ocean waves, by whose side their route lay, which, crested with moonlight, now came up with muffled feet, almost to the wheels of the carriage, and then shrunk back, as in fear — all this conspired to deepen the religious and blissful emotions of their hearts, which had been awakened by the vows they had just spoken at the marriage altar. Of the responsibilities connected with their new relationship, of its perplexities and cares, they thought not now; but rather of the delights of their wedded life, and of the long, uncounted days of bliss that lay stretched before them in the future — a very land of promise. The deepest tenderness was in their hearts, and the most implicit faith in each other; while aspirations after high and good things, that always come to us, in a measure, when we are happiest, grew strong within them.

In pleasant and affectionate converse they

beguiled the short hours of their ride, until they reached the tasteful residence that Hamilton had fitted up for his bride. Then the beautiful eyes of Anna Hamilton brightened anew with delight, and her heart dilated with warmer affection, as she witnessed around her the proofs of love her husband bore her. The utmost deference had been paid to her wishes in the arrangement of their home, and the greatest regard manifested not only for her tastes, but even for her slightest preferences. The very pictures which she had admired at an exhibition of paintings, looked down upon her from the walls; her favorite authors, daintily bound and embellished, lay upon the parlor table; her choicest music was upon the open piano; the plants which she most carefully cherished, bloomed upon the flower stand; the furniture was of the style that she would have selected, and even the hangings of the walls, and the drapery of the windows, were of that delicate shade which would have been her own choice. Love, gratitude, and pleasure, throbbed in her bosom, and when her husband turned to question how her taste was pleased with the arrangements and decorations around her, she buried her face on his shoulder and wept tears of joy.

Few start in life with prospects that promise more of happiness than did Henry and
Anna Hamilton. They were not wealthy,
but riches and happiness, as all the world
know, are far from indissoluble, and they
were in those "easy circumstances" where
dwells the most of enjoyment. Both had
been carefully educated, had been favored
with good advantages, had been accustomed
to intelligent and refined society, both were
young, in good health, were full of life, and
each was devotedly attached to the other
To the world generally, the marriage seemed
an admirable one; predictions of the happiness the wedded couple would realize, were
uttered in good faith, and not as heartless
words, while the married ones themselves
saw before them only a cloudless future.

There were some, however, who knew the
parties better than they knew themselves,
who saw in their characters the elements of
future misery, unless both maintained the
strictest self-government. Ardent, warm-
hearted, intelligent and pleasing, Anna Hamilton possessed one trait of character that
often caused pain to those who loved her,
and suffering and deep humiliation to herself.
She was passionate, or, as we say, quick tem-

pered. Few, out of her own family circle, had ever witnessed ebullitions of the fiery spirit that generally lay dormant in her bosom; for love of approbation, if not self-respect, restrained her, and she knew that it was unlady-like to be seen in a passion. Moreover, temptations to the "sin that so easily beset" her, were few and slight, in the circle in which she moved, where she was seldom thwarted, but was surrounded by those who aimed to please her rather than otherwise. But in the bosom of her own family, and with those intimate and familiar friends, with whom she observed perfect freedom of language and manners, she gave way, when provoked, to startling and frenzied bursts of passion, as terrific as the wild flash of lightning from the summer cloud, when she would recklessly hurl forth words that went through the hearts of those at whom they were aimed, with keener edge than swords, and the memory of which rankled and festered in the bosom long after. In a moment the frenzied girl would become calm, and then she would give worlds to unsay what had just been spoken in passion; would weep bitterly and humbly over her error, and resolve against the besetting sin to which she so readily yielded.

Hamilton's nature was somewhat different. He was far from being what we call excitable, and was not easily roused to anger; but he differed most from his wife, in that while she recovered from her indignation almost instantly, his endured for days; her temper was like the flint, "which, much enforced, shows a hasty spark, and straight is cold again;" while his was the fire of a volcano, deep, smouldering, burning and inextinguishable; he was not easily provoked, but then his anger endured almost forever. He was, to be sure, slow to wrath, but he was also slow to forgive, and to forget, was with him impossible.

How would these dissimilar and strongly marked characters of the husband and wife harmonize when both should be tried by the multifarious cares, duties, trials, and perplexities, which marriage brings more or less to all? Would the wife be led by her love for her husband to practise forbearance and self-government, and would the same potent influence incline him to forgiveness? Or, would the familiarity of constant intercourse produce carelessness of manners, and indifference to pleasing, so that the latent fire of the young wife's heart would burst out

against her husband, when vexed by him,
causing alienation of feeling, and temporary,
if not life-long estrangement?

Days and weeks passed away, and the
lives of the twain were as sunshiny as they
had dreamed they would be. Nothing was
as dear to them as the society of each other
their recreations and amusements were in
common, and their home was indeed a paradise. The return of Hamilton to his meals
after half a day's absence, was welcomed by
his wife as though he had been away a
twelve-month; and their leave-takings, when
he departed to his office, were as affectionate
as though he were bound on a journey.
Nothing had occurred to vex her, or, if it
had, love or a desire to please, had prevented her manifesting it.

Months passed, and the fervor of their
affection had somewhat cooled, though there
was still no lack of love, and then there was
frequently evident in the manner of Anna a
slight degree of petulance, which caused a
seriousness on the part of her husband. She
had become accustomed to him, and had
allowed the first expressions of anger to
escape her, which, though slight, were to be
deprecated as the prelude to more violent
feeling and utterance.

The summer had passed away, and winter had succeeded with its cold and ice, its merry sleigh-rides and lively pleasure parties. ·Heavy falls of snow had been followed by clear, cold weather, and there was a general turnout of all classes to enjoy the exhilarating pleasure of sleighing. Day after day Hamilton had promised his wife "to get up a sleighing party," but as often had his business prevented, and obliged him to disappoint her. At last, however, after a week's vexatious delay, he found a leisure afternoon, and so he rapidly drummed up recruits for the evening's frolic, and made hasty preparation for the entertainment and comfort of the company.

It was a clear, bright moonlight, the sleighing was glorious, the music of the jingling bells filled the frosty air, the fleet tread of the spirited horses over the frozen snow, as they flew here and there and every where to gather up the company, stirred the blood wildly in the veins, and Anna Hamilton, all excitement, and arrayed for the ride, sat at the parlor window, straining her eyes to catch a glimpse of her husband, whom she momentarily expected. But the slow moments moved on, and still he came not. Just

as her patience was tried to the last degree,
and when she had given up all hope of his
coming till too late for the ride, and was
straining every nerve to keep back the tears
that almost gushed from her eyes, Hamilton
dashed up to the door. Springing from his
sleigh, he strode up to the steps, and burst
into the house, panting and out of breath.

"Dear me! I've hurried like the mischief
to get ready, and 'here I've waited, at least
an hour for you," was Anna's petulant greet-
ing. "Pray, what kept you so long? I
thought you'd never come!"

"I began to think so myself," was her
husband's reply. "Thompson, the agent of
the Smithville factories, which have got into
some difficulty, has been at my office all the
afternoon. His business with me can't be
deferred, and it will occupy me till late in
the evening, so that I cannot go on this ride.
It's vexatious, but there's no help for it;
'business before pleasure,' you know. But
I have arranged it so that you can go, and
you must frolic enough for both of us. So,
come, jump into the sleigh, for there's no
time to lose."

"I shan't stir a step," said Anna, throwing herself into a chair, her brow gathering

darkness, and her eyes flashing fire. "I should think you believed me a child, to be disposed of just as you please. I should like to know *how* I can go without you?"

"Why, easily enough; I will drive you to the hotel, where we meet, and consign you to the care of cousin Frank, who is going with his wife, in the six horse sleigh; you are not large, and they can stow you away among them nicely."

"Well, I shan't go; I don't relish being packed away like a bale of cotton. I'll stay at home, as I always have to now-a-days;" and with a most ungracious manner, Anna began to tear off her hat and cloak.

"Oh, now, *do* go Anna!" said Hamilton, coaxingly, hardly noticing her vexation. "I wish I could accompany you, but you see how it is. Come, you *must* go, you have so long anticipated this ride; go, just to please me."

"*Just to please you!*" she repeated, turning on him furiously. "A great deal *you* care about it; you don't care a straw about my gratification, so you can only stay in that gloomy old office of yours from morning till night. I should not care a half penny if it were to burn to the ground."

"Pshaw, pshaw! Anna! now you are un-reasonable," said Hamilton, slightly vexed. "I am so much confined, that for my own gratification, I should like this ride, and much more should I be pleased with it, if I might go in company with you. You are unkind and unreasonable now."

"Oh, fuss! Well, I don't care if I am! I was warned before I was married, of the ob-scurity to which wives are doomed, but I little dreamed that I should be as completely buried alive as I am." And partly from dis-appointment, partly from anger, she burst into tears.

Although her words had irritated Hamil-ton, yet her tears moved him, and he sat down beside her, and putting his arm about her waist, made one more effort. "Now, don't cry, Anna, *don't* I beg you. You had better go on this ride, you will be happier than to stay here alone. After I get through with Thompson, I will drive on and meet you, and perhaps may be able to take supper with you. But *don't* cry so, for I cannot bear to see you unhappy."

Anna, however, was thoroughly angry, and her husband's pleas, instead of calming, only made her more passionate. She seemed determined to rouse him. Shaking off his arm contemptuously, she said with great bitterness, "Pray, don't use any more of what Sam Slick calls 'soft sawder.' If you would speak the truth, you would say you are sorry you are encumbered with a wife to claim the time you prefer to devote to musty law books, and dull old men, and quarrelsome people. I don't believe a word about this visit of Thompson; it's all fudge! But if I ever ask again any favor of you, I hope you will be just as obliging as you have been now — and refuse me outright; that will save you the trouble of inventing excuses. I only wish I was Anna Hastings once more; I'd see if I'd peril my happiness for the soft speeches of any man living."

This angry speech, so undeserved, so unjust, cut Hamilton to the very soul. Withdrawing his arm as though a viper had stung him, and starting to his feet, he stood for an instant, transfixed with astonishment, gazing on his wife; and, then, without uttering a word, he left the house, jumped into his sleigh, and his wife saw him drive away, like one mad, the buffalo streaming out on the wind behind him.

But scarcely had he closed the door behind

him, when an entire revulsion of feeling took
place in the bosom of his wife, and she bitterly repented the rash words she had just
uttered.   She would have given worlds
could she have recalled them.   It was the
first time that he had seen her in a passion,
and she feared that it would alienate him
from her forever.   The current of her feelings instantly took another direction, and
she passed from the frenzy of anger to the
most extravagant grief.   Pacing the floor
hurriedly, she wrung her hands, upbraiding
herself bitterly, and wept wildly and hysteri-
cally.   Such violent emotion soon wears
itself out, and before her husband had returned, Anna had become comparatively
calm, though she was entirely undecided as
to the course she would pursue.   At one moment, she resolved to acknowledge her error
to her husband as soon as he entered the
house, and to sue for his forgiveness, promising never again to yield to an angry spirit;
but the next, she shrank from humbling herself, and concluded to let time wear away
the impression of this unhappy evening.
While thus undecided Hamilton came in.
The heart of his wife throbbed so tempestu-
ously, that it almost suffocated her, tears

blinded her eyes, and she trembled like an
aspen, but did not speak. Neither did he,
but sitting down calmly by the table, he
turned the lamp to get a better light, drew a
newspaper from his pocket, and began to
read. Several times Anna essayed to speak,
but her voice died away in her throat, and
so she sat by the grate silently, shading her
eyes with her hand, and rocking nervously.
An hour passed in this uncomfortable manner, and then Hamilton laid down his paper,
and taking a lamp, made his way to his
chamber.

This abrupt way of retiring was very different from his habit generally; and Anna
listened increduously to his retreating footsteps, till she heard him close the door of his
chamber, and then, in an agony of remorse
and grief, she threw herself upon the sofa,
and wept uncontrollably. How vividly came
to her remembrance the warnings of her
mother, who had bidden her beware of her
first quarrel with her husband! Could she
ever hope to prop'tiate him, whom she knew
to be slow to anger, but almost unappeasa-
ble, when offended? Hours passed away,
and the fire burned out in the grate, and the
lamp emitted but a feeble light — but Anna

14

heeded neither the increasing coldness of the room, nor the waning light; she was absorbed in bitter thought, in dreadful self-reproach, and most harrowing fear. She wept, till she could weep no longer, and exhausted by the violence of her feelings, she sunk into slumber, broken and uneasy, and terrified by dreams. When she woke, the sun was pouring into the half open shutter, violent pain was in her head, she was benumbed with cold, stiff and weary. As soon as she comprehended how she came there, and recalled the unhappy events of the evening before, she rose, and staggered towards the door, with the intention of going to her husband, and throwing herself on his bosom, to seek reconciliation with him.

But at the very moment her hand rested on the door knob, she heard his footsteps on the stairs. "He will surely come into the parlor," thought the poor wife, "for he will see that I have not been in bed, and then I'll ask forgiveness." But no — he passed on through the hall, turned the key in the front door, and went out, not even turning to look towards the parlor windows. He had misunderstood the cause of his wife's passing the night in the parlor, and thinking it but

another manifestation of her anger, was himself incensed by it, and left, purposely avoid-
ing her, and resolved not to return till night.
Anna ran to the window to gaze after him,
and even tapped on the glass, almost involuntarily, to be sure, hoping to arrest his
attention, but he did not hear, and went on.
And again was the miserable wife plunged
into fresh sorrow, and almost into despair;
she struck her clenched hands together wildly, and walked the floor rapidly, not knowing
what to do. For a few moments she abandoned herself to utter despondency, and
almost wished to die.

Suddenly, a bright thought flashed into
her mind; her husband would soon return
to breakfast, and she would therefore make
everything pleasant for his coming, and then
the breach between them should be healed.
Immediately she went to work upon this suggestion; and though her head ached to bursting, and the blood ran in her veins like fire,
she hurried to the kitchen, and assisted Ellen
to broil the beef steak, to bake the lightest
of biscuit, and to make clear and delicate
flavored coffee; and having arranged her
hair according to *his* taste, and dressed in
the morning gown that was *his* especial fan-

14N

cy, she went to the breakfast room to wait
his return.

But alas! the breakfast became cold on the
kitchen hearth, and the hands of the clock
moved on towards noon, and Henry Hamilton was still an absentee from his home, as
he had resolved in the morning when he left.
It was a dreadful day to Anna. The hours
went by like years. Noon came, and then
slowly, slowly came on the night, and she
had not seen her husband. In vague fear,
in terrible suffering, in alternate watching
and weeping, she spent the long day. As
night came on, all courage and hope forsook
her, and she yielded to the physical suffering
which she had been combatting while hope
was in her heart. She had taken a heavy
cold the night before, sleeping on the sofa,
and the blood coursed wildly through her
frame, while the pain in her head almost
made her delirious. Not a morsel of food
passed her lips during the day, and faint and
heart-sick, weak and hopeless, she groped
her way to her chamber. She felt too ill to
undress, and was reluctant to come in con-
tact with the domestics, in her present state;
and she therefore sank on the bed, in the
cold, fireless apartment, when, from exhaus-

tion and illness, she was soon lost in disturbed slumber.

At the usual hour Hamilton returned home, and not finding his wife below, he sought their room. He ascended the stairs, laid his hand upon the door handle, and was about to enter; and then he recalled her angry words to him, her absence from their room the night previous, and turning haughtily away, he said to himself, "No; I'll let her get over her anger in such time and way as she pleases," and entering another chamber, laid down for the night. Had he entered his own room, and seen his suffering wife, lying on the bed in burning fever, unshielded from the biting cold of the night save by her ordinary clothing, tossing, turning, starting and moaning in her slumber, her eyes inflamed by weeping, and the veins of her temples swollen out like cords, he would have pursued a different course. He was now acting under a cruel mistake.

Anna slept on until midnight, and then she awoke. The lamp was burning dimly on the table, the air of the room was chilling, the dreadful pain in her head was more violent, the very flesh seemed burning off her bones with the intense fever that was upon her,

her husband had not yet returned, as she thought, and feebly, hardly knowing why, she again went down to the parlor. All was still, the servants were asleep, the house fastened for the night — all seemed at rest and quiet, but herself. She sat down, and tried to think how she ought to act. She believed that her husband would never return, that he had forsaken her, and that she should never again see him; and connected with this dreadful fact of what she deemed his desertion, was a vague idea, which floated through her mind, that she ought not to remain alone, now that her husband had forsaken her; that she must go away somewhere where she had friends, now that the one friend dearest to her on earth, had failed her. But her thoughts wandered, she could hardly tell at times, even where she was, she could lay no plans, and going from one room to another, now lying on the sofa, now holding her throbbing head, moaning and weeping, she passed the time till daylight. A coach rattling by, on its way to the railroad, freighted with passengers for the morning train, aroused her to consciousness. The sight of the carriage, whose load of passengers and baggage told its destination, brought thoughts of home to her half-crazed brain, and she remembered her mother, and immediately, her determination was formed. "Yes," she murmured to herself, "I'll go to my mother! a mother never forsakes! a mother never ceases to love! never! I'll go home to my mother!" And putting on her hat and cloak, which lay in the parlor where she had left them, on the night of her disappointment about the sleigh-ride, she went out into the street. Fortunately a hackney coach came along, by which she obtained conveyance to the depot, for in her disordered state of mind and body, she would have failed to reach it on foot. The fever that had settled in her system raged more violently, and when she reached her father's house, racked with pain, burning with fever, faint from exhaustion, wild in her manner, and incoherent in her language, they sent in alarm for a physician, and despatched a messenger in the afternoon train for her husband.

Henry Hamilton was as startled by the message that summoned him to the bed of his sick wife, as though a thunderbolt had fallen at his feet. He had believed her at home, sulking in her chamber, and had worked himself into a deep passion with her, for retaining so long her displeasure at a mere disappointment, and fortified by his anger, had held himself entirely aloof from her for the last two days. How was he startled and conscience-smitten to learn the truth, to hear from the trembling lips of her brother that she was at her father's house, tossing wildly on a sick bed in the delirium of brain fever, from which her physician feared she would never recover! He delayed not a moment, and though night had already set in, he hurried as fast as the fleetest horses could carry him, to her bedside.

Agonized, and rent with contending emotions, he sat beside her, day after day, a pale and anxious watcher, while she seemed lying at the grave's mouth. She did not recognize him; but in the wanderings of her delirious fancy, she revealed to him how deeply she loved him, and how much she had suffered from her passion and his treatment of her. Her self-upbraidings; her pathetic appeals to him for forgiveness; her wild woe at his fancied desertion of her; her mournful calls upon her mother for the love and protection her husband had withdrawn; all this pierced his heart, and his hours of watching were hours of almost ceaseless prayer for the preservation of that life now doubly dear to him, and which he resolved ever after to beautify and bless with his forbearance and affection.

Those earnest and penitent prayers were heard in heaven, and slowly Anna Hamilton emerged from the valley of the shadow of death, to consciousness and convalescence. She awoke to reason, to find her husband hanging tenderly and anxiously over her, with affection in his eyes, and gratitude in his heart, and to witness tears of joy rain down his pallid cheek at her recognition of him. Feeble as an infant, she could not obey her first impulse to twine her arms about his neck, and plead for pardon, but deep bliss thrilled her being, as he laid his cheek to hers, and forbidding her to speak, breathed in her ear not only love, pardon, and reconciliation, but prayers for forgiveness for his own sin against her, and renewed vows to ever love and cherish her, and to abjure the revengeful and obdurate spirit that had caused them both so much suffering.

Nor were those vows made in the hours of sickness and sorrow, forgotten in health and happiness. The consequences of their first quarrel were most salutary to both; they were taught by them a lesson of forgiveness

and forbearance that was never forgotten;
and the memory of them, in after life, acted
as a Mentor, when angry words rose to their
lips, and a tempest of wrath was beginning
to gather in their bosoms.

THE TEMPLE OF THE SKY.

"God keeps a niche in heaven to hold our idols."

She was our first and fairest, and I worshiped her
    in pride,
And from death's sway to ransom her, I would my-
    self have died;
For I loved the holy beauty that on her young
    brow gleamed,
And the earnest gaze of softness that from her
    bright eyes streamed.

I drank the broken melody of her half-spoken words,
As she sang at morn and evening, when sing the
    little birds;
And I thought among the angels could none so
    beauteous be :—
Oh, the life of that frail being was every thing to
    me !

But my heart grew faint with anguish that smote
    it to its core,
When they bore her from my bosom, to nestle there
    no more;
I looked upon her shrouded for her long night's
    dreamless rest,

Her white hands folded gently on the marble of her
    breast.

My soul was bowed within me, but I murmured no
    complaint,
No bow of promise in my sky did hope essay to
    paint:
I daily made a pilgrimage to where my darling
    slept,
And the little spot was moistened with bitter tears
    I wept.

There came a dewy twilight hour, and clouds like
    snow-wreaths pale,
Threw o'er the moon advancing slow, a graceful
    misty veil;
My heart was emptied of all joy, and my palsied
    tongue was still,
And there brooded o'er me, raven-like, a hopeless
    sense of ill.

But there sudden glowed around me, a subdued and
    holy light,
Gentle as the day's declining, solemn as the hush
    of night,
Gladsome as the morning's brightness, breaking
    pure and undefiled;
And within the softened splendor, stood my heaven-
    crowned child.

Like a breeze of summer healing, joy went sweep-
    ing through my frame,

With a thrill of strong affection, fondly I pronounced her name;
And I stretched my arms towards her, as to draw
her to my breast,
For I thought my love might win her from the
dreary grave to rest.

But she said in whispered music, "Win me not to
thine embrace!
In the temple of the Holy, God hath given your
child a place:
Where the brightly vested angels, who an earthly
eye would dim,
Chant the music writ in heaven, a divine love
breathing hymn."

"And to grace this beauteous building, from the
world are gathered in,
All the heart's most cherished idols, yet unmarred
by touch of sin;
Fair their spirit-brows are gleaming, in their holy
homes on high:—
Thou wilt find the child thou lovest, in the temple
of the sky."

Outward swung the gate of heaven in the rosy-
tinted air,
And their eyes were beaming earthward, warm with
love, and free from care;
On my cheek, I felt the glancing of a lightly-wafting
wing,
And again, on golden·hinges, back I heard the por-
tal swing.

To my angel-child I turned me, but my spirit-guest
    had flown,
And amid the faded brightness, I, the childless,
    stood alone:
But there's graven on the tablets of my loving,
    yearning heart,
That amid earth's shrined idols, I, in heaven, can
    claim a part.

THE SONG OF THE MOONLIGHT.

I've tinged the fragrant evening air
  With soft and heavenly hue;
I've poured a wealth of mellow light
  Along the sky's deep blue;
And silvered o'er the sleeping earth,
  Bedecked with gems of dew.

I bowed to see the giddy dance
  That's wreathed by billows white,
And as my smile stole o'er the sea,
  They gave it back as bright;
And on the brow of each young wave,
  I left a star of light.

And through the dense and tangled green,
  That towering forests twine,
I sent a brightly gleaming ray,
  Amid its gloom to shine;
It seemed, as downward far it fell,
  Like jewel in a mine.

I placed a diamond, large and bright
  On every mountain's crest;
I lit the dew-drop hid within
  The timid floweret's breast;
And like a blessing, laid my smile,
  On verdant fields to rest.

And where the low-voiced evening wind,
    Was lifting in its play
The snowy folds that draped a couch,
    I, noiseless, winged my way;
And then I kissed the parted lips
    Of her, who dreaming lay.

And round that fair child's holy brow,
    I twined a halo bright;
For o'er her bowed a shining one
    In robes of heavenly white;
And dazzling was the crown he wore
    Of warm and softened light.

And well I knew his mission was
    To take that child to heaven;
For this my crown of moonbeams pale
    About her brow was given;
'Twill fade when worn above the sky,
    As twilight fades at even.

But lo! the rosy-footed morn
    Unlocks the eastern sky;
And crimson rays, with golden blent,
    Athwart the azure fly;
And sweet the morning chime that floats,
    From arch to arch on high.

And so my mission endeth now;
    I seek the sloping west;
Gath'ring this thin and misty fold,
    Of clouds about my breast,
As calmly as departing saint,
    I'm sinking to my rest.